A Mac...
Tu...

A macho pass sudde... ...omplete shift of power, and became *her* kiss instead of *his*. Her taking a mood out on him, instead of the other way around. *His* knees knocking. *His* hands unsteady. *His* lungs begging for oxygen in gulps...when it was supposed to be *her*, bowled over by his experienced sexual prowess.

The damn woman didn't *have* any prowess.

But man...could she kiss! Lexie could make a man believe he was the hottest thing ever to emerge from a *Y* chromosome. The only guy in her universe. The only man she ever needed or ever wanted in her universe. The only man...

Aw, hell.

Dear Reader,

As we celebrate Silhouette's 20th anniversary year as a romance publisher, we invite you to welcome in the fall season with our latest six powerful, passionate, provocative love stories from Silhouette Desire!

In September's MAN OF THE MONTH, fabulous Peggy Moreland offers a *Slow Waltz Across Texas*. In order to win his wife back, a rugged Texas cowboy must learn to let love into his heart. Popular author Jennifer Greene delivers a special treat for you with *Rock Solid,* which is part of the highly sensual Desire promotion, BODY & SOUL.

Maureen Child's exciting miniseries, BACHELOR BATTALION, continues with *The Next Santini Bride,* a responsible single mom who cuts loose with a handsome Marine. The next installment of the provocative Desire miniseries FORTUNE'S CHILDREN: THE GROOMS is *Mail-Order Cinderella* by Kathryn Jensen, in which a plain-Jane librarian seeks a husband through a matchmaking service and winds up with a Fortune! Ryanne Corey returns to Desire with a *Lady with a Past,* whose true love woos her with a chocolate picnic. And a nurse loses her virginity to a doctor in a night of passion, only to find out the next day that her lover is her new boss, in *Doctor for Keeps* by Kristi Gold.

Be sure to indulge yourself this autumn by reading all six of these tantalizing titles from Silhouette Desire!

Enjoy!

Joan Marlow Golan

Joan Marlow Golan
Senior Editor, Silhouette Desire

Please address questions and book requests to:
Silhouette Reader Service
U.S.: 3010 Walden Ave., P.O. Box 1325, Buffalo, NY 14269
Canadian: P.O. Box 609, Fort Erie, Ont. L2A 5X3

Rock Solid

JENNIFER GREENE

Silhouette® Desire®

Published by Silhouette Books

America's Publisher of Contemporary Romance

SILHOUETTE BOOKS

ISBN 0-373-76316-6

ROCK SOLID

Copyright © 2000 by Alison Hart

JENNIFER GREENE

lives near Lake Michigan with her husband and two children. Before writing full-time, she worked as a teacher and a personnel manager. Michigan State University honored her as an "outstanding woman graduate" for her work with women on campus.

Ms. Greene has written more than fifty category romances, for which she has won numerous awards, including two RITAs from the Romance Writers of America in the Best Short Contemporary Books category, and a Career Achievement award from *Romantic Times Magazine*.

IT'S OUR 20th ANNIVERSARY!
We'll be celebrating all year,
Continuing with these fabulous titles,
On sale in September 2000.

One

The Idaho sky was a brilliant blue, the mountain scenery breathtaking, the spring afternoon as seductive as a lover's kiss…and Lexie's heart was slamming with panic.

She'd always loved flying, and this bitsy single-engine Piper was more fun than a roller-coaster ride. Flying wasn't the problem. Her recent bout with insanity was.

For several months now, she'd tolerated these silly symptoms. She was old friends with insomnia; that wasn't new. It was this other stuff. On a perfectly wonderful day, her heart would suddenly pound, her palms turn cold and clammy, her stomach twist and tangle up with nerves. Her doctor had diagnosed the symptoms as an anxiety attack—which was total bullcracky.

She had nothing to be anxious about. At twenty-eight, her life was luckier than a dream—she was making money hand over fist, success charging her way faster than she could keep up with it, her work a joy and challenge both. Every day was filled with a frenzy of excitement, commotion, risk, everything she loved. There was no excuse whatsoever for these sudden attacks of panic…yet she could feel it starting again—the lump of anxiety welling up in her throat, the stupid roiled-up feeling in her stomach, the loneliness of fear nipping and nagging at her normally cheerful nature.

"Hey, you okay, Ms. Woolf?" The pilot of the Piper Cub was named Jed Harper. Jed was quite a character, with his unshaven white whiskers and wrinkled face and Hawaiian shirt. She strongly suspected that the wad in his cheek was tobacco.

"Just fine," she assured him. Or she would be. She'd signed up for a month at Silver Mountain specifically to solve these idiotic health problems of hers.

"Well, we're headed down, ma'am. Be on the ground in five more minutes, now. Silver Mountain's one of the most beautiful places on earth. You're gonna love it."

"Uh-huh." Mountains. Trees. Fresh air. It was enough to make a girl nauseous. Momentarily Lexie closed her eyes, fantasizing about her Victorian office with the red velvet office chair and the draperies dripping fringe and the billowing, delicate Boston fern…and the giant TV in the background with nice, soothing CNBC shooting the ticker tape past every second of the stock market day.

Perhaps this particular anxiety attack was justifiable, Lexie considered. Not only was she suffering from Dow Jones withdrawal, but she considered a stay in the country on a par with grape cough syrup. A tough, strong woman, of course, bit the bullet and took her medicine without whining…but that didn't mean she had to like it.

The baby-size plane hit the grass landing strip, bounced, hit the ground again and finally settled into a jog-skipping-pace before wheeling into a turn. God knew where it was turning. There was nothing in sight but endless sharp, spiked pine trees covering endless sharp, spiked mountains. She saw no buildings, no telephone poles, no asphalt—nothing comforting or familiar.

The wizened-faced Mr. Harper—Jed—turned off the engine, grinned at her and then hustled to open the door. "Now don't you worry about a thing, Ms. Woolf. We handle city folks like you all the time. You'll feel like a new person after a month here. I guarantee it…and here comes Cash now. You're going to love Cash. All the women do."

Lexie ducked under the door frame and climbed down. She wasn't here to love anyone. She was here to get over these anxiety attacks—or die trying—yet her first second in all the blasted fresh air made her stomach buck uneasily. Everything smelled…green. Suspiciously, verdantly green. As if she were in the middle of a jungle of overgrown Christmas trees that just went on forever. This high, this far from anything civilized, the air was so pure it stung the lungs. How was a woman supposed to breathe without pollution? Where was the comforting carbon monoxide, the diesel fumes, the traffic stinks? Where were the malls?

"Hey, Jed. You made record time. And we've been waiting for you, Alexandra—welcome to Silver Mountain."

It wasn't that she didn't hear the warm masculine tenor. For a couple of seconds, though, she was so distracted by the view of all that appalling, petrifying green that she couldn't seem to look away. Swiftly she reminded herself that she was not only willing to be here—she'd paid a fortune to be here—so it was no one's fault but her own if she felt plunked down on an alien planet in the middle of a *Star Trek* episode. Quickly she spun around with her smile on and her hand out. "Thanks, Mr. McKay—Cash. And let's forget that Alexandra business. No one calls me that. It's either Lexie or Lex…"

Her voice petered out faster than a stalled engine. She knew the man reaching out to shake her hand was Cashner Aaron McKay, the owner of Silver Mountain. She'd have known his voice from their telephone calls even if the pilot hadn't identified him, and he'd been so natural and easy to talk with that Lexie had been looking forward to meeting him. Still was. It was just that the blazing sun had first shadowed his face, and from their phone calls, she'd just assumed that McKay would be someone like Jed Harper—someone older. Someone with skin leathered by a hundred million years in the sun who wore cowboy boots. Someone who didn't slap her snoozing female hormones wide-awake.

But now he was closer. So close the sun wasn't blocking her vision. So close that she realized two startling things simultaneously. Her host for the next few weeks was. the Marlboro man come to life—sans cigarette. The hunk was take-your-breath adorable, tall and lean and blue-eyed and downright edible. And the second thing she realized was that she was standing downhill…which meant that the hand she'd shot out to shake his was coming perilously close to poking the hunk in the crotch.

Faster than lightning she yanked her hand up to an appropriate height. Humor seemed to responsively glint in his eyes—not that she had time to analyze his reactions. They did the handshaking thing, which thankfully gave her throat a chance to swallow some of that saliva before she drooled all over him. She'd already resigned herself to the month of torture ahead…but being able to regularly look at McKay was definitely going to lighten her suffering significantly.

"Lexie…" His gaze was direct, the slow grin friendly, but the callused palm that had so warmly gripped hers abruptly dropped. She never sensed any negative vibes, just that he hadn't noticed her in any particularly personal way. Possibly he didn't go for short-haired, sprite-size brunettes with city pale skin. "Glad to finally meet you in person. And I hope you're going to love our Silver Mountain. We'll get your gear, get you settled in. Jed, you coming up to the house for an iced tea?"

"You bet. And where's our favorite hellion?"

Cash let out a low, easy chuckle. "Sammy's still doing that home-schooling we set up out of Hammond's...but he'll be raring home in another hour or so."

"Sammy?" Lexie asked.

"Sammy's my son. Well, I guess technically he's my nephew, but he's my son in every way that matters. You'll meet him at dinner, if not sooner...although he's a little more shy around the women guests. At least you can hope he'll be shy. Otherwise you're at risk of his talking your ears off."

Again, that slow, easy grin. Jed grabbed two of her designer bags and loped on ahead. Cash grabbed four. Neither remarked on the amount or size of her luggage. "That's it, Lex? Anything else you need carrying?"

"No, no sweat." Briefly Lexie wondered what he meant by referring to this Sammy-child as being both nephew and son, but right then she stumbled over a gnarled root. There was nothing particularly new there. She'd always been able to trip on thin air—athletics weren't exactly her strong point—but she really did need to promptly change clothes. Her Italian sandals had been comfortable for flying, but lacked a certain sturdiness for this type of terrain. Worse yet, the hike was all uphill. The strip where the teensy plane had landed was the only flat spot anywhere in sight. A stitch in her side was screaming by the time they'd gone a hundred yards, and the only things she was toting were her purse and laptop. "I'm not too used to exercise," she huffed.

"That's okay, no one is when they first come here. That's the point. That you get a serious break from constant work and the stresses of city life, right?"

"Right." Although no one had warned her about all this ghastly fresh air.

"Even if you're not normally into country life, I think

you'll find it grows on you. There are no bottom lines here, no deadlines, no tests to pass…''

She knew all the reasons why she'd signed up to come here, so there was no particular reason to listen. Besides, she could have looked at his back all day. My. At fourteen, she'd thumbtacked posters of hunks on her bedroom wall like every other hormone-driven adolescent girl. Then, of course, she'd grown up and realized that looks were no measure of character or anything else that mattered. By twenty-eight, she'd come to another realization milestone. Maybe heartache was the pits, but just looking was a lot of fun and didn't cost a dime.

Over the years, she'd tried picking out potential lovers with the same meticulous care she picked stocks—studying assets, start-up costs, long-term growth potential, how long one needed to be patient before seeing a return, that kind of thing. Her analysis methods worked fabulously with stocks. But with men…well, temporarily she'd sworn off gambling with anything so high-risk.

As she told her friend Blair, vibrators were just a whole lot less aggravation.

But that wasn't to say that she didn't enjoy looking. On a scale of 1 to 10, McKay easily had a 10 fanny—and Lexie had always been a fanny type of woman. Still, eventually, she got around to noticing the rest. The flannel plaid shirt looked straight out of L. L. Bean; the boot-cut jeans were old and loose and worn-in like an old friend. His hair was short and as straight as mink fur but tawny, a mix of sun-streaked caramel and butterscotch. Even this early in May, his skin was sun bronzed, that tan incredibly striking against his light blue eyes. He had a man's-man look all day, his jaw looking cut out of stone, the cheekbones jutting out to give him an even more rugged profile. And there was that cute itsy-bitsy guy butt again—

"Not too far, now, Lexie. The house is just around the corner."

"No problem," she sang out. She was loathe to tear her eyes away from the only seriously interesting view—his butt—but around the last curve, the lodge loomed in sight. The big, fat log house stood three stories high, with a wrap-around veranda graced with porch swings and wooden rocking chairs. She clumped up the porch steps behind Cash—stumbled on the doorjamb, but thankfully didn't fall—and then stepped in. Jed had already dropped her two bags and disappeared from sight when the screen door clapped behind her.

Whew. The place made her think of a movie set for a Western oil baron story. The front door led into a square foyer with a giant staircase, but off to the right was a living room with sprawling couches and groups of oversize chairs in forest-greens and honey-leathers. Man-size windows opened on the mountain view, and nests of thick-pile rugs were scattered around. She glimpsed a gaming table in a dark, scarred mahogany. An upright piano. An oil painting on the far wall, almost as big as the wall itself, a mystical painting of the mountains bathed in a morning mist in ghost-whites and whisper-greens and blues.

A stone fireplace dominated the great room, smoke-scarred and full of character. The chestnut floor and oak ceiling beams looked equally well-worn and well loved.

"This is the hangout place in the evenings." Cash led her through, either because they had to go that way, or to help familiarize her with the layout. "If you're bored, you can usually find a game of poker or pinochle going on after dinner. Even summer nights, it's cool enough that we usually light a fire here. Then in here's the dining room...."

She poked her head in, saw an oblong pine table with a million leaves and a wagon wheel chandelier.

"Meal hours are posted in your room, but if you get hungry other times, you can always raid the kitchen on your own. We're not running this place like an inn. We want you to feel it's your home while you're here…with one little exception. Before we go any further, we need to make a stop.'' Past the dining room, he popped a door on another room, this one stashed with the desk and file cabinets of a no-nonsense office. Temporarily he thumped her luggage down. ''Afraid you need to strip here, Lex.''

Not that she wasn't willing—for him—but the suggestion still startled her. ''Did you say strip?''

''Uh-huh.'' His expression was so deadpan that she almost missed the unrepentant twinkle in his eye. ''This room locks up, tight as a bank vault, so you don't need to worry about anything getting stolen. And I don't want to have to do a strip search, but I will if I have to.'' He waggled his fingers in a come-on gesture. ''I'm afraid this is the place where you have to come clean. I want all your loot. Portable computer. Pager. Cell phone. Everything electronic you've got.''

She wanted to chuckle at his strip routine—the devil!—and normally she would have. Just then, though, her sense of humor seemed to be suffering a short gasp. ''Everything?'' she asked weakly.

''Well, if you *have* to have a pacifier, I guess you can take the cell phone to snuggle in bed with. You can't get any reception here anyway, so there's really no harm—but that's it. Everything else gets locked up. If you just can't stand it, you can come in and stroke the computer every now and then.'' Even the twinkle was unrelenting. And those fingers kept saying ''gimme.''

For a moment she stared at him in numb panic. Yes, of course, this was exactly why she'd come. A month forced away from work. A place where she couldn't do business or get into stress no matter how hard she tried. For that matter, she was paying a near fortune for Mr. Cashner Mc-

Kay to take charge of her life and boss her around just like this, so it didn't make any sense to balk. "But you have a TV somewhere, don't you?" she asked bravely.

"Yup. In my living quarters. But nowhere any of the guests can see it."

She was reassured that at least some proof of civilization existed and was close by. Still, she gulped again. "I, um, haven't been separated from my daily dose of the Dow Jones for almost nine years."

"I understand," he said patiently. "One of our longtime guests is a doctor who always hyperventilates for the first few days without his pager. The first few days are the hardest, but I promise, it really does get easier after that. If you panic, I'll let you in here to see your stuff, okay? But I want you to give it a chance."

"Of course I'll give it a chance. In fact, I can't wait to get started on your whole program." But she struggled with him for a minute when he tried to take the lizard computer case. It was like being severed from her own, personal, life-giving umbilical cord. "You have a phone somewhere in the lodge—?"

"Of course we do. Several. You're not really cut off from anything, Lexie. Jed flies in with supplies a couple times a week. Guests come and go. And my private quarters have all the technology you're used to if we need to contact a doctor or civilization or if relatives happen to need you. Now, are you ready to see your room?"

He took her toys. All of them. Even the palm reader. Even the headset for her disc player.

And then he motioned her toward a back staircase and led the way up. "Last week, the place was full—for us, that means ten guests, the max we can handle at a time. Or the max we want to. For the next couple of weeks, it'll be extra nice, though, just you and a few others. Come summer, we'll be extra busy again. Now…the library's on the third floor in the back, and it's well stocked. Workout gym, massage room and hot tub are in the square building off the north—Bubba comes in three times a week to do the masseuse thing. You'll meet him tomorrow, and you'll meet Keegan at dinner tonight. Keegan's working on his Ph.D. as a naturalist, and in the meantime trading cooking and some bookkeeping for room and board. And George makes up the last of the staff, he's the housekeeper...he's a little on the gruff side, but he gets the job done, comes in around four mornings a week and we cope the rest of the time on our own. You leave the house, let someone know. Or check out at the desk in the kitchen. Lots of great places to wander, but we don't want you getting lost...."

The more Cash informed her about the lodge setup, the more Lexie kept thinking: lions and tigers and bears, oh my. Maybe this was a mistake. Back in Chicago, coming here had seemed like such a foolproof idea. Since she was too much of a workaholic to force herself to rest, she'd chosen to go where she simply *had* to. And this place certainly fit that bill, except that she'd never envisioned anywhere so uncivilized that it actually had bears and cougars. And no malls.

"Here, you go." At the top of the stairs, Cash motioned her inside the first room to the west, then stepped in himself and lined up her luggage as obediently as Catholic school children. After that he pushed open the sash of the far window, letting in another gush of stinging fresh air. "Okay now...the bathroom's through that door. Dinner'll be served around six, so you've got some time to unwind, unpack, wander around. If you need anything before then—"

"No, honestly, I'm fine."

"No questions at all so far? You like the room?"

"No questions. And the room's wonderful." She saw the four-poster bed and bureau in wild cherry wood, the country quilt and feather mattress. The bed alone could have slept three people her size. Maybe four.

The bedroom window in her Chicago apartment—her $2,000 a month Chicago apartment—viewed someone else's bedroom in someone else's pricey Chicago apartment. Here she looked out on mountains that were too damn breathtaking to make a picture postcard. Nobody'd believe they were real. Yet somehow she was the one who felt unreal, just trying to look around and believe she could possibly fit in around here.

"Lexie?" When his hand touched her shoulder, she spun around with a city woman's instincts honed against getting too close to strangers. His hand jerked back, yet his shrewd blue eyes suddenly rested on her face, something warm and evocative and completely unexpected in his eyes.

Cash had been nothing but kind and friendly from their first phone contact, and certainly since she'd arrived here. Still, his attitude had been exactly what she'd expected and exactly what it should be—completely impersonal. That he might see her differently from the other city slickers who came to his Silver Mountain hadn't occurred to her...until she suddenly felt his gaze on her face, the connection in his touch.

"You're feeling like a fish thrown in the desert, aren't you?" he asked quietly.

"Yes." There was no point in denying it.

"So did I, once upon a time. But I've been in your shoes, Lex, working so hard and so furiously that I didn't realize I was forgetting to stop and take a breath. And this mountain has magic, I swear. You don't have to be an outdoor person to get the benefits...you don't ever have to do anything like this again, either. But we both have the same goal—not to send you back home until you feel rested and recharged again. Okay?"

"Okay," she said, and decided then and there that she was in love with him.

Having only known him for less than a half hour, of course, she didn't exactly mean a death-defying type of love—but she wasn't looking for that, anyway. She'd come here expecting the next month to be a penance, though, and instead McKay was not only kind and perceptive, but as a bonus, he had a quick sense of humor. Maybe the next few weeks weren't going to be as terrible as she'd dreaded.

Once Cash disappeared downstairs, she opened suitcases and closets, pushed off her sandals and started settling in. Yet only minutes later, she heard the distant high-pitched squeal of a child, and she wandered over to the window to investigate.

The boy bounding up the mountain path, yelling for Cash, was easy to identify as a McKay. He had Cash's same tawny hair and long legs. The urchin was maybe eight? Nine? Not so old that he cared a hoot if his hair was wind-tangled or his jeans dirt-dusted from the bottoms up.

And right below her bedroom window, Lexie suddenly saw the child leap in the air—obviously trusting without question that he was going to be safely caught. And Cash was suddenly there, swinging him around and high as if the boy weighed nothing. She heard the child's joyous, "Guess *what*, Cash? *Guess what?*"

And then Cash's low, rumbling laughter before both of them lowered their voices and ducked out of sight.

For a few moments, Lexie couldn't seem to budge from the window. Something old and aching swelled in her throat, the way listening to an old love song could trigger potent longings sometimes. There'd been so much love and laughter in Cash's voice…and so much trust and love in the little boy's voice, the same way.

With a sudden impatient sigh, Lexie pushed away from the window and forced herself to finish the unpacking job.

There was no excuse for letting that longing feeling get to her. God knew, she'd been blessed in her life. Sometimes, though, as much as she adored her adoptive parents, she still remembered her mom and dad, remembered that kind of secure, natural, joyous love, remembered feeling as if she belonged. Once upon a time, she'd been a fearless, sassy kid who'd never doubted for a second that she owned the whole world.

She was still fearless. Still sassy—or so the investment guys she worked with regularly teased her. And she'd always been loved, even if she had lost her real parents at a vulnerable young age. But somehow, since that time, she'd never gotten back that feeling of belonging.

As she finished the last of her unpacking, her gaze drifted around the room, from the oil lantern on the bureau to the rag rug to the big, varnished door with the thick brass latch. It was a good, sturdy room. Comfortable. Safe-feeling. But she didn't belong here any more than she did anywhere else. And at twenty-eight, sometimes, the feeling of loneliness just seemed to overwhelm her.

Lexie headed for the door, doing what she always did when old, disturbing shadows started chasing her. She thought about money. It was the one subject on the planet that she was unquestionably fabulous at. Making it. Hoarding it. Amassing it. Other women dreamed of lovers. Lexie dreamed of taking a bath in silver dollars, luxuriating naked in all that cool, smooth silver, letting it rive and flow and tickle and cool her overheated skin.

Sure, love was nice. But when you lost people, it ripped out your soul. Money was far more effective security. Lose some money, and there was always more to be made.

Of course, for the next few weeks, she was stuck in this godforsaken wilderness and couldn't make a dime. But as she glanced at her watch and then headed downstairs for dinner, she thought that at least there was no possible threat to her of any kind here—unless one could overdose on too much fresh air.

And both McKay males looked as if they were going to be interesting company and a lot of fun.

No worry for her, in any possible way.

Two

Talk about trouble.

Cash scooped up another serving of lasagna, even though he'd barely tasted the first serving. All through dinner he hadn't been able to take his eyes off Ms. Alexandra Jeannine Woolf. Any other time, that big name of hers would have amused him. The first time he'd heard it—on the phone— he'd unconsciously assumed that she'd be physically substantial like the size of her name. Instead Lexie couldn't weigh much more than a sack of potatoes...but that wasn't to say she wasn't one potent female package.

One *worrisome* potent female package.

He'd already inhaled the physical details. Lips like ripe-soft peaches. Eyes like luscious, liquid chocolate. Nothing exactly unusual about her hair—it was short and wildly curly—but the color was a glossy raven-black, a striking contrast to her porcelain pale skin.

Cash gulped down some iced tea. He'd been baby-sitting

executives and business hotshots for almost a decade—long enough to recognize the labels she was wearing. More men than women came to Silver Mountain, but the women who chose to stay here invariably had The Look. Expensive. Tasteful. Whatever they wore, you never saw on anybody else. And nothing, naturally, was ever practical for outdoor mountain life.

Because he never forgot his responsibilities, Cash glanced around the dining table. A half hour before, dishes were heaped groaning-full, scents steaming around the long trestle table. A quiet was starting to fall, though, as the group filled up. Instinctively he picked on his shyest guests and said something to Mr. Farraday—the banking mogul seated to his left—and then something else to Stuart Rennbacker, the CEO on his third stay at Silver Mountain, who was still wolfing down the lasagna as if there was no tomorrow.

Cash wasn't about to neglect the guests, and dinner was when everyone loosened up and got to know each other. Still, part of his attention never left Lexie.

For the third time since dinner began, she dropped a fork. On this cool May night, she was wearing a white angora sweater that snuggled her breasts better than a guy's fantasy...but no pricey sweater was going to help make her unklutzy.

She laughed at something his son said, and Cash felt his stomach clench. Not with nerves—because he was never nervous—but with worry.

Maybe she was wearing two-hundred-buck slacks, but there was nothing about her laugh that sounded snobbish. She was skinny, short and built skimpy upstairs and down—which, damn it, happened to be his favorite shape on a woman. Even more aggravating than that, she laughed from the belly. In fact, her laugh took up her whole face, crinkled her eyes, showed off a mouthful of superb white teeth—except for the tiny crook in her eyeteeth, which actually only made her look more adorable. And that damn laugh could make any guy's head spin around—even if it weren't for the cute little boobs and the dark-chocolate eyes and that sexy mouth. She laughed like she meant it. She laughed like she loved life. She laughed like she would exuberantly let go once the lights were out with the right man.

Get a grip, McKay.

He tried. He said something to Farraday and Rennbacker again—then Whitt, one of the guests who was leaving tonight. By the time his gaze strayed back to Lexie, she was dribbling a forkful of peas, half on her plate, half on the floor, because she was bent down, giving all her attention to his son. She didn't care about the peas. She looked straight at Sammy when she talked to him. Other people didn't always do that to a kid. Grown-ups—especially the executive type of upper class grown-ups—had a habit of saying nice, polite things to a child while their eyes wandered around the room seeking more adult interests. Not her.

She liked kids.

Hell, Cash thought morosely. She wasn't just a little trouble. She was potentially Serious Trouble.

He never had to warn himself to be careful around women. The female of the species had always been the bane of his life. That wasn't to say his hormones couldn't go into a wild tailspin for a woman with looks and brains—and brains were usually his worst downfall. He *did* turn on for a woman with a quick mind. But he was thirty-four, after all. Women-battle-scarred enough to recognize heartache before it had the chance to level him.

His weakness, though, was how people treated Sammy. And Lexie, so far, was treating Sammy like he was the most terrific boy she'd ever laid eyes on. As if the kid were more important and more interesting than anything or anyone else on the planet—which he was, Cash thought. Only what that half-pint brunette didn't know was that Sammy never—repeat, capital *n* Never—took to a strange woman.

Sammy, at age eight, was as woman-battle-scarred as Cash was.

Suddenly Keegan stood up at the far end of the table, his ponytail neatly clipped at his nape, a kitchen towel hooked in his belt loop in lieu of an apron. "Anyone up for dessert? I've got a big fancy chocolate mousse. Or a blackberry pie."

Although Lexie demurred from dessert, the others nearly rioted with enthusiasm—no surprise. Everyone except Lexie knew that Keegan could bake dirt and make it taste delicious. The kid was being wasted, working on his Ph.D., when guys were paying a fortune for someone with his old-fashioned wife qualifications. But once dessert came in— typically—the room instantly quieted down, which enabled Cash to watch her in action with Sammy again.

And again, worry started pumping adrenaline through his veins. It wasn't that he minded her talking to Sammy in any way. The problem was that the inconceivable was happening. Sammy was actually initiating conversation with her, too. And seemed happy to be talking to her besides.

Cash had to strain to catch some words, and finally hooked into part of their conversation. Lexie was obviously answering a question.

"Well, sure, I've got a picture of my family that you could see…just a second." When she started digging in her wallet, naturally, her napkin whisked down to the floor. Then a spoon dropped.

Sammy filched the photo she handed him, and then blinked in surprise. "Like this is your mom and dad? Are you kidding? You look way different than everybody else."

Cash happened to accidentally glance over just then, and he blinked, too. Usually there was nothing exciting in anyone's family photos, but this one really was startling. The snapshot framed a family picnic in suburbia somewhere, summer, a hot day, with Lexie sitting cross-legged on the grass. She was flanked by four people her own age—two young men, two young women—and then two older adults standing up. Everyone looked related except Lexie. The others were all Nordic blondes, unusually tall and noticeably athletic and broad shouldered. And then there was Lexie—small, slight and dark, a changeling with those exotic oval-shaped eyes....

"Well, Sammy, the reason I don't look like them is because we're not related by blood. I'm adopted. I lost my mom and dad when I was really little, like three years old."

"You're adopted?" Sammy repeated, making Cash immediately tense, his slice of blackberry pie forgotten. She had no way of knowing this was an uneasy subject for the kid, but he did.

"Yes, hon."

"So...what happened to your mom and dad? Did they die or leave you or what hap—?"

"Hey, champ." Cash's voice was as lazy and easy as a western summer breeze, not clipped, not showing even a trace of nerves. "I'm sure Ms. Woolf understands that you're just being curious, but it makes most people uncomfortable to be asked personal questions. You can ask her where she lives, stuff like that. General questions."

Cash tried never to duck a parenting issue just because there were outsiders around, because outsiders were around their lives all the time. So when he had to correct Sammy, he did his best to teach and explain a reason rather than to make him feel criticized. This time, though, Sammy wasn't up for hearing any lessons.

"But Cash, I just wanted to know how she got to be adopted—"

"It's all right," Lexie said swiftly, before Cash could say anything else. And to Sammy, she bent her head again. "It's not a secret or uncomfortable thing for me, hon, even though your dad's right. It could be for some people. But I don't mind answering you. My mom and dad died. They were killed the same night in a robbery—and it was pretty terrible—but after that, a wonderful family took me in, the Woolfs. They loved me as much as my first mom and dad did, and I love them enormously the same way, so everything turned out just fine.''

"Well..." Sammy shoveled in a giant spoonful of mousse, some of which even made it inside his mouth, while he seemed to think this over. "I wasn't just being curious. I was int'rested because I'm almost an orphan, too, only not exactly. I never had a dad. 'Course, I never wanted a dad, either.''

"No?" Lexie asked gently.

"No. Because I have Cash, and nobody's dad could ever be better'n Cash. It's just us guys against the world. We can do anything because we help each other.''

"That sounds really wonderful." Again, Lexie's voice had softened to butter.

"Yup. It's wonderful. But I can't be an orphan like you because I have a mom. In a way it's the same, though, because you lost your mom, and my mom doesn't want me. Sometimes she calls and pretends to be nice and all, but she never comes here. What I think is, I'm so much trouble that she just doesn't want nuthin' to do with me—''

Swiftly Cash scraped back his chair and stood up. "Well, I want you, champ. In fact, I couldn't run this place without you. Come on and help me in the office for a minute, okay? If you'll all excuse us.''

Sammy charged into the office, his face all lit up as if he were hot-wired to a joy button. Come hell or high water— or work—Cash spent private time with the boy every day, and before Sammy spilled any more private family information to strangers, he figured it was a politically good time to do their male bonding thing. Not that he was protective of Sammy…but he'd have used an elephant gun on a mosquito that dared threaten the boy. And not think twice.

So first, there was Sammy-time. And then he had to sit down with Keegan to go over the week's schedule. After that, George was driving Whitt into Coeur D'Allene, which meant that Whitt's bill needed settling and the guest seen off and George given directions. Then the bills needed to be pawed through. Hell, there was always a ton of stuff that needed doing at the end of the day.

But the new guest preyed on Cash's mind. It wasn't because he felt any unsettling, special pull for her—at all. In any way. But Sammy seemed to, and Sammy hadn't talked to a woman like that in three months of Sundays. Probably longer. And since it was her first day, it was natural enough that he'd try to track her down and make sure she was settling in.

Only she wasn't in her bedroom.

He tried the lodge living room, where the boys were playing pinochle. When he didn't find her there, he checked the barn, the gym and hot tub building, the general grounds. Sammy had been stashed in bed by then, tucked safely in their private quarters, Cash wearing a pager so the squirt could always reach him…but in the meantime, he was running out of places to track down Lexie.

Eventually he found her—on the third floor in the library. When he first poked in his head, he saw the lights turned on, but no sign of a body. Once upon a time the library had been an attic, but he'd put up skylights and shelves and then a widow's walk balcony with a mountain view. From then on, the room had become a favorite for everyone. Sammy had unearthed the one-horse sleigh in one of the old barns—which was completely worthless as a sleigh—but they'd fixed it up together to make a couch-type seat for reading. The old claw-foot bathtub was stuffed with giant pillows—that was Sammy's favorite reading spot. And most of the men seemed to either pick one of the Abe Lincoln rockers or one of the clunky, chunky Morris chairs. Not her.

There was no hearth or wood-burning stove up here, because the threat of fire was too high, but Cash had wired in abundant electric heat and added rugs to warm up the place. It was her feet he spotted first. They happened to be naked feet, distinctly girl sized, with the toenails painted a candy-apple red—such a sassy, sexy red that he *had* to grin. There was just no way this one was ever gonna go for a flannel-shirt type of lifestyle.

He strode in and peered over the couch edge, his gaze tracking the trail of bare feet waving in the air to where she was lying flat on her back on a scruffy old rug. She'd bunched the couch blanket under her head, making it into a pillow, and her expensive white sweater and fancy slacks looked as out of place as china at a rodeo.

"You had to lay on the floor? All the chairs too big for you?" he asked humorously.

"What can I say? I've always been a floor-sitter." She smiled at him over the spine of a beaten-up old book. "Were you looking for me?"

"Not to bug you if you're happy reading. But I wanted to be sure you were settled in okay." Hell, his pulse was already rattling from just looking at her. Those small breasts disappeared completely with her laying flat, but there was just something about that lithe, compact body that made his hormones buck. It wasn't some out of control thing. He was no adolescent. But damnation, there was something about her that really soared his wings.

"I'm settled in fine. Although I'm glad you stopped by. I was worried about you."

"Worried about *me?*" Cash hunkered down in one of the Morris chairs, leaning forward, not getting too comfortable—but the idea that this half-pint city vamp could have worried about him couldn't help but arouse his sense of humor.

"Yeah." She eased up to a sitting position, leaning back against the old corduroy sofa. "I picked Silver Mountain carefully. You have an outstanding reputation. The way I heard it, even the most burned-out, exhausted executives leave here feeling recharged and reenergized. Two of the men claimed they felt as if you'd shaved ten years off their lives."

"Big exaggeration," he said wryly, "but you'll get some experiences you can't get in an office. I promise you that."

She nodded. "I like your whole program or I wouldn't be here. But I'm afraid you're going to fail with me. And I don't want you to feel badly when that happens. It won't be your fault."

He raised his eyebrows. "How come you're so positive the program isn't going to work for you? You haven't even given it a shot yet."

"And I will. Believe me, I'll try two hundred percent. It's just that I've never been able to do anything athletic...so I don't want you to worry that your teaching skills or your program ideas are at fault. It'll just be me screwing up. Not you."

Well, if this wasn't a damnably strange conversation—but she'd sparked his competitive spirit now. She was right. He *hadn't* failed with anyone yet, and he certainly didn't intend to start with one half-pint brunette. "How about if we don't worry about failures or successes quite yet? We'll just take it slow, see how you do tomorrow."

"Okay. Sure...although maybe I should mention—the only thing I just know I couldn't handle in your program is the mountain climbing."

"Heights aren't your thing, huh?" He cocked his head. "A while back, maybe last year, I think I saw an article about you. The Pixie with the Midas Touch, something like that?''

She winced. ''Man, I hate that label. But yeah, that article was about me—except that the journalist slanted it to make me sound way more hotsy-totsy than I am. I started investing in the stock market when I was fourteen. Just birthday money. Nothing extraordinary. But somehow any stock I bought developed this nice habit of doubling, until that 'Midas Touch' tag started to follow me around. I couldn't shake it. Anyway…'' She motioned around the library, as if hustling to divert the conversation away from herself. ''This is an incredible home you have here. Was the lodge in your family? Is that how you happened to create this retreat for executives?''

From a stranger, he usually minded nosy questions. But not from her. He'd specifically tracked her down—not just to feast his eyes on that sassy mouth or skinny little body. But to clear the air on where he was coming from—and find out for sure where she was. ''Yeah, the house was in the family. My great-gramps trekked to Idaho back in the Silver Rush. There's still a petered-out silver mine on the property, although it was never worth much.''

''So you grew up here?''

''Yes, although not by choice. When I was a kid, the only thing on my mind was city lights and getting out of here. But we lost both my dad and my gramps in the same logging accident, so I grew up as the only male around. My grandmother gave me a sense of honor I couldn't shake. Family first. That was her cardinal principle, and about the time my mom died and left me the property, I was stuck with it. No point putting it on the market—who in his right mind would want to buy it? There's nothing up here but mountains and eagles. And I was living in Boise then, making good money—and spending it even faster. In fact, that's how I got my Cash nickname, because I never could hold onto a dime. And to tell you the truth, I never cared.''

The start of a smile tugged at the corner of her mouth. She was enjoying the yarn spinning. ''So the lodge was in your family...but you had absolutely no reason to want to be here.''

''Exactly. Except that I have one younger sister, Hannah. And somehow she missed all the family lessons about that honor-first business. She got pregnant with Sammy. Took off to find her so-called fiancé after Sammy was born and it seems she still hasn't found him, because Sam's eight now and he's still with me.''

Compassion seemed to soften and darken her eyes. ''I loved watching you two together. You're obviously close.''

''Cut-and-dried, there is nothing I wouldn't do for him. He may only be my nephew, but I love him like a son.'' He used his drawling, lazy voice. Reliably that tone tended to relax people, which helped when he had to say something tough. ''Somehow the place has turned into a real male bastion. I swear I'd hire women—there's no reason in hell the staff has to be all male—but there just doesn't seem to be any females dying for jobs in this neck of the woods. And yeah, for sure, we have women guests, but they're only here for a short time. Which is why I brought this subject up, so I could tell you the lay of the land as far as Sam. He can be a little sensitive around women.''

''He's a darling.''

''Yeah, I think so. But with females, he's not long on trust. He just doesn't believe any woman is going to stick around for him. The guests come and go. His mother's flightier than wind. And when I saw him talking to you at dinner—''

''You got worried?''

''Not *worried*. But he doesn't do that. Warm up to women strangers the way he did with you. He usually avoids all females like they had cooties. So if he starts to form an attachment, I'm just asking you to be careful. He acts like a pretty tough little kid, and he is. But he can still get hurt.''

"I'm glad you told me.'' Her eyes met his. "Just for the record, I'd shoot myself before deliberately hurting a child. Just in case that was the message you were trying to get across in that gentle way of yours.''

She cut her gaze away from his so fast that Cash felt a sharp slash of guilt. "Hell. Did I hurt your feelings? Keegan says I'm as subtle as a sledgehammer on my good days.''

"I was teasing you, not complaining. And it wouldn't matter if you hurt my feelings or not. I'd do the same thing in your shoes—say whatever needed saying to protect a vulnerable child in my care. I loved watching the two of you together.'' Swiftly she glanced at her wrist. "Good grief, it's almost midnight. I'm keeping you up, and me, too. I just came up here to find a book.''

She grabbed the book, then uncoiled and leaped to her feet, then swooped back down—apparently—for her shoes. Cash saw her suddenly flying around, but when he stood up from the chair, she seemed nowhere near him. He wasn't exactly sure how a shoe suddenly hurtled out of her hand. Or why the book dropped. Or how the crown of her head somehow managed to ram into his chest, throwing both of them off balance.

Instinctively he grabbed her, his hands closing around her upper arms until she steadied. And she steadied fast enough, but she was still red-faced and laughing when she tilted her face.

"Cripes, I'm so sorry. I warned you I was clumsy, didn't I?''

"Don't worry about it—um…'' She started to bounce down to reach for the fallen shoe again, and almost jabbed a sharp elbow in his crotch. Startled, he grabbed her arms again—as gently as he could—and tried to tactfully lift her a few inches safer distance from him. "How about if you let me get your shoes and the book? And don't move for a second."

"Scared I'll do you injury, huh?"

"I think you've got incredible potential as a defensive end. Although I'm afraid defensive ends don't usually come in your size."

She chuckled. But then her laughter faded. As if someone flipped a switch, Cash was suddenly conscious of the sudden hush in the room, the dark shadows and intimacy of lamplight, the scent of books...and her perfume. It wasn't pixieish and gamine like her, but a soft, sexy, exotic scent, spices he didn't know, flowers he couldn't name. The perfume made him uneasy, but that wasn't why he shifted on his feet.

An embarrassed rose was still brushed across her cheeks from her near tumble. But at that second, her face was still tilted toward his, her lips barely parted, those liquid chocolate eyes fastened on his face.

He had the craziest sensation that she wanted to kiss him. Or to be kissed. By him.

That first lunatic sensation was followed by another. He wanted to kiss her. The way he hadn't wanted to kiss a woman in forever. Not a let's-get-it-on kiss. Not a hi-there-honey kiss. Not a let's-test-these-waters kiss.

But a kiss that communicated *Damn, I've been waiting for you forever. I didn't know I'd ever find you. I really didn't believe you even existed. Not for me.*

His throat was suddenly too dry to swallow, his pulse galloping like a colt's in spring. He couldn't remember ever having this stupid a reaction to a woman. Naturally, though, he recovered swiftly, smiled, moved. Especially moved. "Well, you're not going to have any trouble finding your way back to your room, are you?"

"I don't think I've memorized the whole layout, yet, but I know I can find my room, no problem."

"Well, I'll see you in the morning then, Lexie."

"I'll turn out the lights—"

Again she spun around, so fast—again—that her incredibly lethal elbow almost landed a hook in his ribs. "I'll get the lights, don't worry."

"Did I—?"

"No, no, you didn't do a bit of harm. I just don't want you walking in the dark in an unfamiliar place. I'll follow you in a minute, and clip the lights off after that."

But he lied, Cash mused. She was harm. He couldn't explain how she'd done that ooga booga thing with him a few moments before, but for damn sure, he didn't respond to *normal* women that way. Something about her was different.

And worrisome.

Three

At 6:29 a.m., Lexie's right hand poked out from the cocoon of blankets, lifted midair and waited. When the alarm clock buzzed 6:30, her palm slammed on the sucker almost before it had a chance to screech.

Blearily she opened her eyes. She was used to insomnia, used to surviving for days on end with short-sleep. She was also used to getting up at insanely early hours. But she wasn't used to dreaming about strange men, and it put her off her stride.

She swung her legs over the side of the unfamiliar bed, switched on the light, winced at the glare and then tested her body for complaints. A lack-of-sleep headache pounded in her temples. Her feet hurt from too many hours of traveling the day before, wearing impractical shoes. The muscles in her neck were painfully tensed from too many hours of tossing and turning. All in all, Lexie figured she should be good and miserable.

Instead, an image of Cash McKay pounced in her mind like a charge of fresh, delightful, invigorating lightning. Instantly she forgot all the creaking body parts—or else they self-healed with amazing speed. She couldn't wait to get up and see what the day brought.

Yikes. The terrifying thought bounced through her head that she was losing what little mind she had left.

By the time she'd slipped on pale jeans, a pastel shirt and new hiking shoes—the leather soft as butter—she was scowling...and feeling more like herself. How could she possibly be looking forward to this day? If she were at home, by now she'd have made three phone calls, checked her home fax and inhaled early-morning CNN before her teeth were brushed. She didn't know how the Dow or NASDAQ had closed yesterday. She could hear birds, but not a single sound of anything electronic anywhere. It wasn't natural.

She wasn't going to make it here four weeks. Heck, she wasn't going to make it four days.

And downstairs, there he was—and not just Cash, but his sidekick. Actually, through the thick red-stone door of the dining room, a number of male bodies were milling around the laid-out buffet, but it was only the dad and son team who snared her attention. One of them was practicing spelling words for a test that day, and all Lexie could think was how adorable they were, both in worn-in jeans and dark long-sleeved T-shirts and boots, both with a cowlick, both with the same swaggering walk. The pair of them could have a matching sign on their foreheads—Cash and Son, two against the world, no women wanted.

Since she wasn't looking to be a woman in anyone's life, Lexie felt unsure why the two McKays put such a darn lump in her throat. They were just so...darling together. So fierce. So obviously a family, with love they wore like a protective shield. They so obviously belonged together and watched out for each other. But then the one with those sexy, battered eyes spotted her in the doorway.

"Morning, Lex, come on in and grab a plate. You met Slim Farraday and Stuart Rennbacker last night, didn't you?"

She greeted both the guys, and yes, she remembered them from dinner the evening before. Slim was the banking mogul, a little man with kind eyes of around sixty who walked with the frailty of someone who'd recently been ill. She'd instinctively wanted to mother him, and they'd had a great time talking capital gains and futures the night before. Stuart was on his third stay at Silver Mountain, and was a blustery, gruff man in his forties, with the look of an executive and worry built-in around the eyes. They'd both been welcoming to her yesterday, but since it'd been a long sleepless night, she wasn't capable of being friendly until she'd mainlined a couple cups of the obvious.

"Sorry, babe, no coffee."

She spun around at the sound of Keegan's voice. Judging from looks, the scruffy-faced kid couldn't be more than a few years younger than her, but Lexie felt as if she were worlds older in life. Keegan was just one of those perpetual-student types of people. Sweet. Idealistic. Full of good cheer and endless ideas— which meant he was annoying first thing in the morning. She narrowed her eyes. "What do you mean, no coffee?"

Keegan motioned to the tray he was carting in from the kitchen. "I've got a high energy drink made for all of you. It'll give you all the zoom that coffee does but without any of the negative side effects. Trust me, you're going to love it."

On a scale between grape cough syrup and castor oil, Keegan's high energy drink fell about in the middle. Disgusting. And it had no caffeine. In spite of the bulging buffet table, the offerings were primarily granola and fruit. No eggs

Benedict, no toast slathered with guava jelly, no nice, fattening, cholesterol-stuffed doughnuts. Ten minutes later, Lexie was hustled outside with the guys, her stomach whining from starvation and deprivation both.

She wasn't into nature—and didn't want to be—but even a hard-core morning grump couldn't help but savor this one. A lake cupped between two mountains gleamed like sterling silver in the morning sunlight. A whisper of fog danced around the trees, the scent of wet pines so strong it was almost a perfume. Squirrels scampered out of their path. A deer frolicked so close that Lexie tripped and almost ran headlong into a tree because she couldn't stop staring at the darling. And the sky was downright scary. It was such a stinging-fresh blue that she suddenly realized how long it'd been since she'd been anywhere that city pollution hadn't grayed and diluted the sky's natural hues.

The best part of the view, though, was watching their leader. Cash hiked the group up a hill so steep that Lexie started suffering oxygen deprivation…but she still felt the emotional tug that she'd experienced the night before. She'd loved how he'd confronted her about Sammy—it wasn't about her personally, she understood that, but about anyone who could potentially hurt the boy. She loved his protectiveness, loved the look in his eyes when he talked about Sammy, and yeah, she'd liked that personal pull between the two of them, too.

He hadn't kissed her…but he'd wanted to. And she hadn't kissed him…but she'd wanted to. It had been a long time, if ever, since she'd felt that kind of rope-tug for a stranger—particularly for someone so completely unlike herself.

Right then, though, he was herding his minigroup in a circle. "Okay, everybody…Lexie, you're our new man today but as you'll discover, we start every morning the same way, with some kind of problem-solving exercise. It's kind of a way we warm up together, and first, we pair up. I'll work with Stuart, and Lexie, you pair up with Slim Farra-day…Slim really knows the ropes.''

Lexie immediately smiled reassuringly at the frail-looking Slim, thinking nothing sounded too tough so far. The "prob-lem-solving" business sounded interesting rather than ath-letic, and surely anything that Slim could physically do, she could do as well? She pushed up her pastel shirt to the el-bows as Cash continued talking.

"Okay. Lexie and Slim, this is your problem for the morning. You see the creek beyond the trees there?'' Of course they saw the creek. Impossible to miss anything so dazzling in the infernal morning sunshine. "All right. You two have a half an hour to get to the other side of it. That's all you have to do.''

"Just hold on a minute, Geronimo." Lexie waved her hand to catch his attention. "There's no bridge. And you didn't give us any tools or ladders or anything—''

"That's right," Cash affirmed. "In fact, that's the point. You're going to have to use whatever you can find in nature to solve the problem.''

Hands on hips, Lexie wandered over to the dazzling creek in question. The water was so clear that she could easily see the creek-middle had to be waist deep. The distance couldn't be eight feet, more like seven, but still too far to jump, and certainly too challenging a distance for Slim to try jumping. One dip of her finger announced that the water temperature was sub zero—if that warm—so wading across was com-pletely out of the question.

Mr Farraday sidled up next to her. "Cash always seems to give us what looks like an insolvable problem. But every morning so far, we've managed to find some way to solve it in spite of ourselves.''

"And we'll solve this one, too," Lexie assured him. She'd made her first paper million before the age of twenty-two, hadn't she? How hard could it be to cross a little creek?

And Cash—the cad—was already out of sight. Some gentleman he turned out to be, pairing the two husky macho
guys, and leaving an undersized Ms. Klutz with Mr. Frail.

"I know we can do it," Mr. Farraday affirmed, and then
scratched his chin. "But…how?"

"Hmm…" Again, she pushed up her sleeves. Her system
was still offended at being deprived of caffeine, CNN and
her ticker tape, yet somehow her pulse was picking up a
charge. Challenges had always been one of her favorite
things. Inexplicably it made her feel…safe…when she took
on something that was supposed to be impossible for her to
do.

Firing up on the problem, now, she motioned to the woods
behind them. "God knows, I've been tripping over fallen
branches since we started walking this morning…so how
about this. Slim, you scout out the longest branches you can
find. Don't lift 'em. I'll lift 'em. And we'll just make ourselves a bridge out of the fallen branches, secured by those
rocks in the middle of creek…and then we'll just walk
across. Piece of cake, right, partner?" She lifted her hand.

Slim gave her a gentle high-five. "Right, partner."

When Cash heard the sound of a female shriek, he took
off at a dead run—knowing, of course, who had to be doing
the shrieking.

He charged around trees and brush, barreling to the creek
edge…only to see Lexie—still caterwauling—sitting on her
butt in the middle of the creek, soaked right up to her neck.

Even as he clomped in the water to fetch her, he was
mentally shaking his head. There was a *reason* he'd paired
Lexie with Slim this morning for this particular problem-
solving exercise—and blast it, the reason was that she
couldn't fail. The only logical way to cross the creek was
to make a bridge of branches—and the terrain had the whole
winter's worth of down pine branches to make that easy.

And they'd done that. Made a darn secure little bridge across the water. And Slim Farraday, with no problem at all, even with his arthritic hip, had made it to the other side with no difficulty.

But then there was Ms. Klutz.

"Cash! Help me! I'm going to die of hypothermia! It's so cold I can't breathe and I can't move and I can't—"

"You're not going to die and it's not that cold." He bent down and grabbed her. For a drowned rat—and a miniature-sized drowned rat at that—she weighed a ton. The branches and mud in her hair didn't help. And when she hurled her arms around him in a monkey-hold, she almost tipped both of them back in the water—not to mention that her soaked, clinging body completely drenched his in two seconds flat.

God knew why he had the sudden, desperate urge to kiss her. There wasn't a hormone alive that could conceivably wake up in these temperatures or conditions, and his mind wasn't on sex but on frustration. The first exercise he gave clients was always intended to give them a feeling of success and confidence, and he'd wanted that even more for Lexie, because she'd been so damn clear that she already expected to fail. Only damnation, *no one* had trouble with this exercise. Ever. Before. Her.

"I'm freezing, I'm freezing—"

He knew. He could feel her tight, wrinkled nipples, through his drenched shirt and hers. He could feel her fanny under his hands as well, maybe even feel her goose bumps. God knew, she was clutching him tighter than glue. "I know you're cold. But you're going to be back at the lodge and climbing in warm, dry clothes in ten minutes, tops, I promise. And after that, you partner with me," he said irritably. Hell, his teeth were starting to chatter now, too.

"With you?"

"Yeah. With me."

She lifted her chin so she could look in his eyes. "Um,

Cash? This was my fault. Not yours. I told you I wouldn't do well with the program, didn't I? I don't do well with anything physical. It's just reality—''

Maybe it was her reality, but it wasn't his. Any other client who'd taken a tumble, he'd give them the morning off, let them soak up some sunshine with their feet up. But a principle was on the line here.

Cash wasn't sure what the principle was, but there had to be one. He hadn't built Silver Mountain into a first-class executive retreat by letting clients fail. That was part of it. His whole program was based on making sure every dad-blamed exhausted executive got something good out of it, and he sure wasn't breaking that record for her. And somehow she'd done something to him so that he couldn't get his mind off her. That had gotten tangled up in the principle, too.

Bottom line was, an hour later, Keegan had been sent out to handle the program for the others, and Cash was fresh-showered, dry-clothed and pacing the front lobby, waiting for her. Spare minutes after that, Lexie bounced down the stairs, wearing a new pastel pair of jeans and another cute little pair of tennies and what looked like a raw-silk shirt to him—even if the pattern was a country plaid. Her hair was dry already—how long could it take to dry a couple of inches of bouncy curl? And she was smiling up at him before he'd even had a chance to erase his scowl.

"Okay. I'm warmed up and ready for the next torture," she said lightly.

"Good." He didn't fill her in on the next plan until they'd hiked a good distance up the mountain. She spotted the outside climbing gym, but obviously had no idea what it was.

He unlocked the storage shed and started gearing up, first choosing the right helmet and harness for Lexie, then sorting through the obvious hexes and cams and lobster claws for the exercise…but he kept a wary eye on Lex. He knew she wasn't going to go for this easily. Temporarily, though, the view just seemed to both bewilder and confuse her. She'd perched her hands on her hips and kept spinning around.

"This is the strangest thing I've ever seen. What on earth are all those ropes and poles and boards for? It looks like a playground in the sky," she joked.

"That's exactly what it is. A playground in the sky. It's where we teach the ropes course, the basics of mountain climbing." He motioned to various sites over their heads. "There are about thirty different exercises you can do up there. The climbing wall is just what it looks like. So is the rope ladder. But then there are other spots, where you can practice using anchors and belaying techniques—"

"Whoa." Her smile died faster than a switched off faucet. "Double whoa. Cash, didn't we talk about this yesterday? I'd never have come here if I wasn't serious about giving your whole program a go. Just because I'm lousy at athletics doesn't mean I'm not willing to try almost anything. But climbing is honestly different—"

"Yeah. So you said yesterday. Climbing was the only thing you didn't want to do." He tried fitting a white helmet on her head, only to discover that it was way too big. He clipped back to the shed for the children's sized helmets.

"Yes. For real. Because I'm afraid of heights."

"I understand." The red helmet fit her perfectly, even if it did smoosh down the riot of dark curls. Those soft dark eyes staring up at him were bleak with dread. "That's exactly why I want you to do this, Lexie. Because you're scared. When you came here, you agreed that I'd be the boss, remember? And I'm not asking you to try climbing to make you miserable. I'm asking you because of what happened this morning."

"You mean my falling in the creek?" she asked in confusion.

"Uh-huh. I gave you the easiest exercise we have. And

you flunked it. So now we're going to try the opposite—
giving you something that's tough for you. And you're not
only *not* going to flunk this one, you're going to ace it.''

''Uh, Cash. I don't think so. In fact...see my hands?
They're already getting sweaty. And my stomach. Even
thinking about heights is making my stomach turn over. The
thing is...''

She never finished that sentence. She stopped talking
when he started fitting the climbing harness on her. There
was nothing suggestive about putting a helmet on her head—
but the harness was necessarily more intimate. She was fully
clothed in jeans, of course. But each leg had to be fit in a
stirrup, and secured around her upper thighs. He did the
securing.

Then the harness had to be worked over her hips and
secured at her waist.

He did that securing, too.

He'd done it for a zillion women. And men. It was part
of his job, for Pete's sake. It was one of the ways he could
guarantee a client's safety, because he supervised the equipment use every step of the way. Only that's what he was
always thinking about. Safety. Not thighs and fannies. Not
specifically the way her slim thigh tensed when he buckled
the harness snug. Not specifically the way his knuckles accidentally brushed against her pelvis. Not specifically the
way his fingers curled around the harness as he adjusted the
leather around her hips and fanny. Not the way her eyes
suddenly shot to his when he adjusted the buckle at her
waist.

Since Lexie seemed to have quit breathing altogether,
Cash figured he'd better finish that sentence for her. ''The
thing is...rock climbing is about trust. Not blind trust.
Proven trust. There are different kinds of rock climbing, Lex.
What we're doing isn't 'free' climbing. It's called 'technical'
climbing.''

She didn't answer. When she looked down, though, to where his hands were still fumbling at her waist, she very likely saw his zipper jutting out as if someone had stuck a long, smooth rock in his jeans. Well, hell. It was a knee-jerk biological response. Nothing a guy could help. How could a man possibly touch a woman like Lex and *not* feel a volatile response?

"Technical climbing is especially about trust," he said gruffly. "Because I'm going to be attached to you with equipment the whole time. You're afraid of falling, right?"

Suddenly she was looking straight in his eyes and not an inch lower. "Yes."

"So that's what we're going to do, Lex. You're going to climb up a bit, and then we're going to make you fall. Only I'm going to be attached to you with equipment the whole time. Nothing dangerous is going to happen. There is no possible way I would let you get hurt, do you hear me? And I'm going to prove that to you. Because when you fall, I'll be there for you."

Somehow anything he said seemed to be coming out wrong—as if he were talking about falling in love instead of falling off rocks. And there was this look in Lexie's eyes that amounted to a violent "no" no matter what he was talking about.

"It's not that I don't believe you, Cash. I do. I met you and I trusted you on sight," she assured him. "Only I'd rather eat snails than be suspended from any height. Look. Maybe I'm just not cut out to even try your program. Don't take it personally. It's not—it's me. I'm fabulous with money, it's my thing, but get me around anything physical—"

He never meant to kiss her. Didn't even know he was going to do it. It was about her trying to be funny about being scared. It was about his feeling bad about her falling in the creek. It was because she'd gotten Sammy to talk to her yesterday, and because she looked so cute in the helmet, and because he was already turned on from fitting her in the harness stirrups, and…hell. He didn't really have a clue why he reached for her.

He just did.

She must have guessed a millisecond before it was coming because her lips parted—as if in shock. Or as if she planned to say something. As far as Cash could tell, Lexie had something to say about almost everything.

That was about the last coherent thought he had for quite a while.

She tasted like something expensive and forbidden and desired. Her lips…nothing was that soft. Nothing in this life. Although the morning had been cool, now there was the barest breeze in the air, sweet and heavy with spring scents. The scent of longing. The scent of young dreams. The scent of yearning.

It wasn't that Cash forgot that every single damn woman in his life had caused him nothing but trouble. It was just…he didn't care right then.

There was a hush in the air. It was coming from her. There was a drumroll of need pounding in his pulse. It was coming from her. There was a willingness floating through his bloodstream, a willingness to do something damn stupid— like get involved with her, a woman who was leaving no later than four weeks from now…and that was rashly assuming she made it four days. But the desire punching him in the gut suddenly made all that common sense seem no-account foolishness.

Amazing. That he'd needed her all this time and hadn't known.

Amazing. He pushed off the helmet and got his hands in her hair—amazed that he'd survived this long before giving in to such a fierce need. The texture of her wily, unruly curls, the look of the silky sunlight on her cheek, the sound of her sudden yielding sigh…ah, hell, there was no analyzing any of it.

He took her mouth and then again, tasting her, sampling her, then coming back for the whole feast. Tongues touched tongues, then tangled. He swooped her closer, half lifting her, not trying to be crude, not wanting to be, but if he couldn't feel her breasts and pelvis layered intimately against him, he wasn't positive he'd managed to survive another second.

Those small, slim hands suddenly willingly slid around his neck. Another sigh whispered from her throat, caught between kisses, trapped between kisses. She was still wearing the leather climbing harness, which in no way inhibited movement but only protected her from danger. Only they weren't climbing now, and he had no harness to protect himself, not when she surged up on tiptoe and robbed him of a kiss that he wasn't necessarily planning to give away. She could convince a saint to take up sin. And oh, man.

She was good.

Sunlight speared in the middle of the forest, washing them in that magic light. He didn't give a damn. His work—forget that, too. The two clients finished their morning exercise, the lodge, the hills, his missing sister, Hannah—he didn't care about any of it. When he finally yanked his head up to haul in some air, he wasn't sure where he'd just been—where *they'd* just been—but it sure as hell wasn't his Silver Mountain lodge in Idaho.

He was going to worry about that kiss. A lot.

But he didn't have time to worry quite then. Just then he looked at her flushed cheeks and damp, soft lips and vulnerable eyes, and he not only felt higher than a kite but as macho as a cougar in spring.

"Okay," he said firmly.

She was still breathing hard, but then she blinked in confusion. "Okay…what?"

Darned if he knew. It was the only word he could get out.
It was tough talking past the hormones screaming up and
down his nerves. "Okay," he repeated even more gruffly.
"We're going to make this work for you. Climbing is about
trust. Now, damn it, *trust* me. I swear nothing is going to
happen that could hurt you, or that you don't want. Just give
me one shot at proving that to you."

"Yes, Cash."

Well, maybe he should have kissed her before this.
Clearly that's all he had to do to make her quit thinking and
talking both. She gave him no more objections about trying
out some mountain climbing, no more objections about anything. Guys in the Middle Ages never even got obedience
to this extent.

Only he was so damned rattled he figured he was lucky
that he didn't walk straight into a tree.

Four

Considering that every single bone in Lexie's body ached from a nonstop day of physical exercise, she expected to sleep like the dead.

Instead, as the bedside clock edged toward midnight, she was still battling insomnia. Rather than counting sheep, she was mentally counting kisses—Cash's kisses—which seemed to be only unsettling her worse.

Momentarily she even imagined hearing a sound outside her door, like a little whine or cry, which was ridiculous. This whole wing of the lodge was quieter than a tomb. When the sound didn't repeat, she impatiently resumed chewing on a thumbnail and staring at the midnight shadows in the ceiling, reliving—yet again—exactly how she'd ended up in Cash McKay's arms.

She'd *told* him that she was afraid of heights. She'd *told* him. Yet she'd actually managed to climb about two feet of that petrifying climbing wall—whining "Cash, I can't! I can't!'' every footfall. Cash seemed to feel the project was a failure, but he didn't understand. Climbing six inches for her would have been a success. Two feet was equivalent to conquering the impossible.

And she knew, of course, how the son of a sea dog had gotten her to do it. He'd kissed her. So thoroughly that he'd rattled her wits—and that was precisely the confounding part that had Lexie's nerves in shreds. Kisses were nice, but they were, after all, just kisses. She had no memory of any guy inspiring her to skydive without a parachute before.

McKay was adorable, of course. But that was no reason to come apart in his arms like he was her body-and-soul mate.

And she'd fallen in love with him on sight, but that was no motivation for anything, either. Even speaking of love and McKay in the same breath was a joke. He was seriously a good guy, loving with his son, protective and caring with others. Naturally she'd fallen in love with him, but it was the same way she adored marshmallow sundaes with chocolate ice cream.

Once exposed, one was inclined to indulge and enjoy.

That didn't mean one went stark raving out of one's mind. Cripes, she just might have stripped to the buff if he'd asked her. Actually made love. Outside. In the sunlight. With all that exhausting fresh air.

Maybe there was a drug in Idaho's air, she worried. Something invisible but potent. Something addictive. Or possibly she was suffering from pollution withdrawal, where an overdose of clear air and lack of city pollution caused the brain to freak out from overstimulation. There were all kinds of justifiable excuses for behaving like a dimwit. The problem was finding one she could believe....

But then she suddenly heard another odd noise. A faint scratching.

Exasperated now, she swung her feet over the side of the

bed—my God, the floor was *freezing*—and padded over to the door to listen. There it was. The vague scratching and whining sounds. She flipped open the lock and opened the door just a peek's worth.

Before she'd even had the chance to look down, a wet nose had pushed its way past her knee, and a second later there seemed to be a full grown golden retriever leaping onto her bed.

Once she turned on the light, she added an adjective to her visitor's appearance. The tongue-lolling canine on her bed was a full grown *pregnant* golden retriever.

"For some incredible reason," she asked the dog, "did you think you were going to sleep on my bed tonight?"

The girl's tail thumped a hundred exuberant miles an hour.

"We don't even know each other. And just for the record—I don't even sleep with strange boys, so believe me, I wouldn't consider it with dogs. And why would you pick me, and this particular bed?" Lexie snapped her fingers. "Oh, I get it. We're the only females on the premises, is that it? Everywhere else there's that teensy reek of excessive testosterone?"

She turned off the overhead and switched on the gentler bedside lamp. The yellow glow pooled around the dog's glossy coat. Lexie hesitated, moving closer, but carefully. The eyes were so warm and friendly that it wasn't possible to fear the dog was mean, but she really was pregnant. *Big* pregnant. And if Lexie had been that pregnant, she was positive she'd tend to be temperamental. "Look, sweetie, it's not that I mind your sleeping here exactly, but are you going to be mad if I turn over in the middle of the night? I'm sure you wouldn't mean to bite me, but after all, we don't know each other. I just don't think this is a good idea. And isn't someone going to worry if they can't find you?"

Almost on cue, she heard the thunder of small footsteps

racing toward her room, then silence, then another unexpected nose poked through her door. "Lexie, can I come in? I'm looking for— Oh. You got her. Martha, I've been looking all *over* for you!"

"I take it she belongs to you?"

"Oh, yeah." Sammy vaulted onto the bed to cuddle his dog, wearing sweats so huge that Lexie strongly suspicioned they belonged to an adored male role model, because they sure weren't his. "Cash got Martha for me a'cause she was gonna have puppies and nobody loved her. So now I love her. And Cash has been telling Keegan that this is a great 'portunity because I'll see a mama stick around her young and that'll be good for me. All moms just don't take off on their kids, you know."

"I know, sweetheart." A soft, cushy lump seemed to settle in her belly. She couldn't help falling for Sammy, but tarnation, that blasted lump was partly forming for Cash, too. Damn man. She loved the way he loved his honorary son. "Hey, Sam?"

"Huh?" The freckled face turned toward her, even though Martha was still washing the entire side of his face— lavishly. Lexie had to grin. But as much as she was enjoying the company, she couldn't help noticing the bedside clock.

"Are you always up this late—nearly midnight? On a school night?"

"Oh, I went to bed at eight-thirty. That's really way too early for someone as old as me, but like Cash says, what are you gonna do? I have to be up really early, because it's a long drive to where we do our home-schooling thing."

Lexie noted that he ducked her original question. She hesitated before asking further or prying, Sammy barely knew her. And she shared Cash's concern that she wasn't likely a good person for the boy to get close to. Still, she felt an intrinsic kinship for a fellow orphan, some kind of sixth sense that he might just want to talk to someone. Gently she asked, "Something bugging you, that you couldn't fall asleep even this late?"

He glanced at her, then back to his dog. "It's not that. It's that I don't like to sleep."

An invitation to talk, if ever she'd heard one. "How come? You worried about something?"

"Well, yeah. I guess. A little." Again, his eyes shied swiftly away from hers. "I don't like to go to sleep, because sometimes something happens. And I can't help it. So I just try to stay awake as long as I can."

The way his fingers clutched the retriever's fur, Lexie sensed what he was afraid of. And her heart clutched in empathy at that small, proud chin. "When I was a little girl, I had this little problem with bed-wetting," she said casually. "Don't tell anyone, okay? I was so embarrassed. But it only happened to me this one year after I lost my mom and dad. I thought my adoptive parents were going to give me back because they wouldn't want me if I did anything like that. But they didn't seem bothered. And then the problem went away and I never had it again."

"Are you telling me a story, or did that really happen to you?" Sammy asked suspiciously.

"It really happened."

Sammy started rubbing the mama dog's tummy before talking again. "Well, Cash took me to a doctor. I don't mean the kind of doctor who gives you shots. I mean the kind you talk to. And he said I was upset about my mom not loving me. But I'm not."

"No?"

"I don't care if she loves me. At all. And Cash says just forget it, it happens to kids sometimes, no big deal, so we have to wash some sheets, so what? But I still hate it. I just wish I could be sure it wouldn't happen anymore. And it doesn't all the time. Hardly at all now. But still sometimes.

So I hate to go to sleep.'' A frown. ''You're not gonna tell Cash I'm still up this late, are you?''

''Hey. Do I look like a tattletale to you?''

Sammy looked her over good. ''Well. You don't look like a tattletale, but you do look like a girl.''

''Um…is that an insult or a compliment?''

He didn't seem inclined to answer that. ''You lasted a whole day. I didn't think you'd make it this long.''

Neither had Lexie. But once she scooted Sammy and the golden retriever back to their own rooms, she stared at the ceiling again, feeling more unsettled than ever. These days she rarely had a chance to be around kids…much less to kids who captured her heart as fast and completely as this one had.

But the pull she felt for Sammy wasn't half as dangerous as the increasing tug she felt for Cash. Technically there was nothing wrong with her liking the two McKays, but Lexie never easily got close to people. She was friendly, but she always guarded her heart against loss. In this case, there was no fear of loss at all. She couldn't possibly fit in to the McKays' lives, so there was no possible threat.

As long as she didn't come to love them.

Seven days now. She'd been here seven whole days and Cash still couldn't seem to take his eyes off her.

He hefted an apple from the bowl on the breakfast table and bit down hard, thinking that if he understood her better, he could shake this obsession. There was something about her. Something that disarmed and confused a man when he was around her. Something worrisome. And he wasn't the only one with the problem.

He bit off another apple chunk, his gaze peeled on Lexie and the squirt. She and Sammy were shoveling in breakfast, heads bent together, talking and giggling like a pair of long-lost magpies. Again. In fact, Sammy was talking to her as if she were Wonder Woman personified—which was terrific, Cash told himself. An eight-year-old kid was too young to be a misogynist. About time Sammy got the idea that a female influence in life could be a good thing.

But he didn't need to get attached to a woman who wasn't going to stick around. Damnation, neither did Cash. And imagining Lexie choosing the country life-style long-term was like picturing the New York Philharmonic set up in the Badlands.

It wasn't going to happen.

As it happened, Lexie wasn't the only troubling problem developing around Silver Mountain recently. Cash finished off the apple, watching Sammy's hand suddenly drop beneath the table edge. Martha was huddled at slugger's feet. Both boy and dog looked the picture of innocence, as the retriever kept accepting goodies from Sammy's hand. The one thing Cash had been firm about—from the start—was that Martha had to sleep outside and there'd be no begging allowed at mealtimes.

Damn dog had never slept outside. Even the first night. And she begged like she had a Ph.D. in the dog-acting profession. "And you're getting so fat," Cash murmured. "*When* are you gonna have those puppies, girl?"

That made Lexie glance up. "I think the more important question is *where* she's going to have those puppies."

He heard her, but for that millisecond her comment never registered in his brain. She was smiling at him. It was the same smile that had tangled him up inside and out all week.

He hadn't touched her since the rock-climbing exercise. Nothing like guilt to make a man behave. She'd survived the exercise, but no thanks to him, because she'd clearly been petrified from the get-go. Hell, that was supposed to be the point. Once she understood how the safety gear worked, she would see for herself that there was nothing to fear. Forcing her to try was supposed to prove to her that she was safe with him.

Only it hadn't worked. She'd done what he asked her to do. Darn woman had more spirit and determination than brains. He'd called off the exercise when he realized how miserable she was. He'd misread and failed her both, and blast it all, she *was* safe. In all senses. That was precisely why he hadn't kissed her since.

But damn, it was still there. The lush, edgy memory of those kisses. Those feelings. Even looking at her made him want to smile. Since she'd ruined two pair of Italian shoes since coming here, she was currently wearing an old pair of Sammy's running shoes...which looked laugh-out-loud funny next to her red square-necked top and sueded blue slacks and stylish scarf. And along with the kid's old tennies, her hair was getting wilder by the day. He could picture her waking up next to him with that wildly curling hair. And that small, soft mouth. And that smile, just for him.

Suddenly Cash realized that Sammy was staring at him curiously—and so was Keegan. It seemed he'd left the conversation hanging, something about their pregnant golden retriever, and Lexie chuckling about where the dog apparently planned to have her pups. "You think you know where she's going to have to her puppies?"

"Well, no, not for sure. But Sammy and I have both noticed that for some unknown reason, Martha's developed this attachment to my room. She's always trying to sneak in. We figured it's because she either knows I'm the only female company around...or because she wants to have her puppies in a nice quiet room away from most of the noise in the house...and my room is super for that. Or Martha seems to think so."

Cash frowned. "You two should have told me about this before. Lexie, I really apologize—I never meant for any guest to be stuck with our dog."

"Believe me, I'm not stuck. I'm crazy about her." With a smile chockful of innocence, Lexie's hand accidentally dropped under the table edge, with the same sneaky technique Sammy used. Martha lucked out with yet another tidbit. "But I am a little worried that I'm going to wake up one morning and find a bedful of pups."

He chuckled with her, but he also caught the conspiratorial wink Sammy shot her. Every time he turned around, those two were together. Lex could outtalk any bigwig he'd ever had when she got going on capital gains and Greenspan and all those alien money terms, but when Sammy came home from school, Lexie tended to disappear from sight…and so did slugger.

Breakfast was winding down, and when Sam bounced up from the table, Cash automatically followed him into their private quarters. For the most part, Sammy was more than old enough to get himself ready for school, but there were certain things that just needed checking. Like that his cowlick was flattened down. And his pants were zipped. And that he remembered to take his lunch.

"One more week of school, but then I can be home and helping you full-time, huh, Cash?"

"You bet." A swipe with a washcloth took care of the milk moustache. "Anything special happening today?"

"Nope. School's boring."

"No tests?"

"Well, yeah. But nothing important. Just a dumb test in subtraction."

"Piece of cake, huh?" Cash slicked down his hair one more time, then hesitated. "Hey, champ. You seem to like talking to Lexie."

"Yeah. She's okay. She's funny." He giggled to illustrate. "She's been trying to bribe me."

Cash's eyes narrowed. "Bribe you? To do what?"

"Every day at breakfast, she's been offering me money.

She wants me to turn on the tube and tell her what the Down Jones number is.''

"Dow Jones,'' Cash corrected him.

"Yeah. That's what I said. Down Jones. She offered me fifteen bucks this morning. The deal started out at two. I figure she'll go to twenty.''

"Excuse me? You're milking one of my paying guests?''

"Sheesh, Cash. I'm not gonna take her money. She's just really funny about it. And did you notice she fit in my shoes?''

"Yeah, I noticed you loaned her an old pair.''

"She wears all out-to-dinner clothes. Except for my shoes. And you know what? She *likes* my shoes.''

"Uh-huh.'' The more the kid talked, the more Cash could feel worry tickling his nerves. "Sammy…you talk to her as if you really liked her.''

"Yeah, I do.'' His eyebrows lifted. "I thought you liked her, too. She's pretty and funny and all.''

"Yes, of course I like her.'' More than he'd expected. More than he understood. "But she's…extra city. Even compared to the other females who come here. And she's only going to be here a few weeks.''

"I know that.'' Sammy looked exasperated. "But she's such a klutz, Cash. And she can't even tell north from south. I think she needs us. She's an orphan, did you know that? She got adopted and all. But the way you and me have each other…she just doesn't seem to have anybody like that.''

Once Sammy shot off to school, Cash found himself restlessly pacing around, unable to settle down to work quite yet. The kid's intuition just got to him, because he'd sensed the same thing—that Lexie didn't have anybody. Adopted family, yeah, a big business life, too. But no one to just talk to, or she wouldn't be hanging with slugger as if spending time with the kid was more precious than Tiffany's gold for her. And Cash didn't figure she'd kiss like she'd been deprived of decent kisses, either, unless she'd been alone for too long.

Somehow, though, he was thinking about her too much—as if she could matter to him and Sammy. As if she *did* matter. When all he had to do was pace around a few minutes to recognize how completely Lexie would never fit in their lives.

Their private quarters consisted of four rooms; more than ample space for him and Sammy, considering they used the lodge kitchen and all the other lodge rooms and facilities. Before Lexie, Cash always thought their setup was ideal for him and Sam, from the baseball glove on the kitchen table to the boot scuff marks on the coffee table. He took care of stuff—like all their clothes were clean—but there were probably about four loads on top of the dryer, begging for some invisible housekeeping-fairy to show up and fold 'em.

Maybe most of their decor was in browns and blacks, but those were colors guys didn't have to worry about getting dirty. Maybe their mugs didn't match, but they had a state-of-the-art entertainment center. Maybe their underwear was a little threadbare, but they both had sports equipment to die for. So there were still dirty glasses in the living room from the night before—but they had the best computer setup that money could buy.

There was nothing wrong with the life he was providing Sammy with. Nothing. And nothing wrong with his life, either, Cash thought defensively…but every darn thing he recalled that one morning made him feel like he was missing something in his life. Like…

Her.

It would have helped if everybody didn't keep bringing her up. Cash had no time to waste on a dang fool raggy mood, yet getting the workday started didn't help. Typically Keegan checked in with him before making the usual weekly supply trip to town but Keegan had added lemon meringue pie and pink tissue paper and fresh pineapple and a pile of other stuff just because he thought it'd appeal to Lexie. Then Bubba rapped on the office door. Typically they talked over the masseur/gym schedule a couple times during the week but this morning Bubba just wanted to know how come their one female guest wasn't taking advantage of the facilities. And then came an exhausting half hour with George.

Ten minutes with George would have tested a saint's patience, and a half hour without either of them yelling was a rare event, but this morning was worse than usual. The part-time housekeeper was only fifty-five, but he had a patch over one eye, and a wizened arm tucked next to his side—one problem left over from a bar fight, the other from a stroke. Try to give him any sympathy, though, and George would bite your head off. Truth to tell, George bit everybody's head off on a good day—except for Sammy. He thought the sun rose and set on Sammy, which was the sole reason Cash put up with his bad temper.

"I'm just saying it has to have been a year since the windows got a clean. I'm not sure we could see a bear in the front yard through the smudges."

"Well, yeah," George barked defensively. "So they need a clean. Who's arguing with you? But I can do it myself. No need for you to hire any stupid strangers."

Again, Cash strove for patience. "There are too many windows for you to do alone. And God knows, I don't have time. Nobody here has the spare time. If you don't want to hire a window crew to come in, then I will."

"The hell you will," George snarled. "You want the damn windows done, I'll do 'em myself. Who's the boss around here, anyway?"

"George. Could you try to remember? *I'm* the boss."

"Like I care. I'll do the dadblamed windows if I want to. And speaking of that girl…"

"What girl?"

George rolled his eyes. "Since there's only one girl here, you know exactly who I mean. And I just thought I'd get around to telling you. She's okay."

That left Cash temporarily speechless. An "okay" from George was equivalent to winning the Publishers Clearing House sweepstakes. And since that seemed all George wanted to say on the state of the world that morning, he flicked on the vacuum cleaner full blast. George had only turned into a housekeeper after the stroke, and though he'd never been much on dusting, he was heels on wheels with an industrial strength vacuum.

Cash fled. It was time to start the program this morning, and he told himself the fresh air would knock the kinks out of his mood. They'd been booked solid all week, with a group of brokers in from Cleveland on one of the four-day programs, and Cash had been pouring on the coals to keep 'em happy. Still. The problem ragging on his mood came full-slap by the time he got outside and corralled the group together.

George and Keegan and Bubba. His house. Sammy. Even his whole client list for weeks now. There'd been a familiar, constant, comfortable level of testosterone.

Only then he spotted Lexie, and it was like being hit with a tornado—and not a regular, ordinary old tornado, but a blockbuster whirlwind of estrogen. Pure, undiluted, delicious, raw estrogen in its most potent form.

Naturally, since breakfast had been a whole two hours ago, she'd already changed clothes. Now she wearing pale blue jeans. The matching navy-blue top had pale blue piping. Pale blue thingees dangled from her ears. A bitsy bracelet with blue teardrops glinted on her wrist in the morning sun. She'd put on some kind of sex-red lipstick, and she was laughing at something one of the guys said—that unique belly laugh of hers that could force Scrooge into grinning back because he just couldn't help himself. He saw the crinkly eyes at a hundred paces, the scent of her...and no, hell, he couldn't smell that damn perfume from one hundred feet away but he knew she was wearing it, which was almost as bad. The skimpy breasts, the spare slope of her hip, the way she made pure-girl hand gestures...

Cash loped toward the group, thinking hell and then double hell. It was nine in the morning. Work was on his mind—work that he loved, and on a morning smudgy with clouds and so sweetened with spring air that he could have died and gone to heaven. His whole life was going full-tilt-great and yet here he was, harder than rock. Because of a perfume he couldn't even smell.

Something about the woman was destroying his mind. It was downright terrifying.

"Well," he said heartily, "everybody ready for our first exercise? I promise, you're going to have fun with this."

"Fun? Does that mean it involves bugs, sweat, dying of exhaustion and rocks?" Lexie asked.

"Even better than that." Cash had to bop her on the head—she was asking for it—and the others always cracked up over her teasing. "I hate to tell you this, Ms. Smarty-Pants, but this is one exercise that even you're going to love."

"I love all of them," she assured him. "I'm just never sure whether I'm going to survive them."

The others laughed, and so did Cash, but then he got down to business. "Okay, y'all, I need you to break up in pairs. John, you hook up with Gary. Mel and Steve, pair up, then Tim with Skully...and Lex, you stick with me."

"I thought you'd given up on me as a partner."

He'd tried—because a man didn't expose himself to Chivas if he had a weakness for scotch, but the truth was, the damn woman couldn't seem to walk without bruising herself or tumbling or damn near breaking her neck. Nobody got hurt on Silver Mountain. Nobody. He never challenged a group with anything that was dangerous or risky—it would have been a denial of every goal he had for the place. People were supposed to go back to their jobs feeling renewed and recharged, not recovering. They were supposed to have new confidence in themselves, eyes opened a little wider to the possibilities.

And that meant Lex, too. Which meant he had to be the one to pair up with her. Sink or swim, there just was no other choice.

"So what's the deal this morning?" Gary, one of the Cleveland brokers, stepped forward.

Cash pulled out a handful of handkerchiefs from his work pack and started passing them around. "First, I want one person in each group to put on a blindfold. But don't start getting your hopes up that this is something kinky. I'm afraid you'll have to do that kind of thing on your own time. This is strictly for a mental turn-on, not a physical one."

Cash had said the words before. They always got a laugh and the men chuckled this time. But he didn't. The instant he imagined himself blindfolding Lexie, he suffered an instant turn on—and there wasn't anything mental about it.

Five

Lexie started tapping her over-sized tennis shoe. Maybe Cash thought blindfolding someone else was a mental exercise, but where she came from, a man doing that to a woman had his mind on the erotic potential. And so did the woman.

But Cash hadn't quite finished his lecture for the rest of the group. "You hear the word 'delegate' a hundred times in business. But it isn't that easy to trust someone else, now is it? Yet that's exactly what you're going to have to do this morning. I want each of you to spend a half hour in the woods blindfolded. I want you to experience how things smell and taste and sound when you can't see. I want you to exercise those other sensory muscles. And in the meantime, I want you to experience what it feels like to trust someone else to keep you out of harm's way…we'll meet back here in an hour, okay?"

Yeah, yeah, yeah, Lexie thought wryly.

She got it. Just like she got all the other exercises Cash put them through in the morning. He really was tuned to the business mind. This wasn't just about some wilderness retreat that forced a bunch of couch potatoes—such as herself—into the blasted fresh air. He had this exasperating way of making them look at their regular life problems with different eyes.

And actually, it was just what the doctor ordered. She hadn't had an anxiety attack in several days now. She was starting to eat like a pig, might even get up to a hundred pounds if she maintained this level of gluttony. And an occasional ten minutes passed before she worried about the advanced decline ratio or index futures and options. She'd found herself daydreaming over a butterfly—which seemed a sign she was making fabulous progress.

But being alone and blindfolded with a guy she was attracted to just didn't seem like the same kettle of fish. The other stuff was all *restful*.

Cash was as restful as a stallion around a vulnerable mare.

When the rest of the guys wandered off and the sound of their conversation and laughter faded away, she felt Cash's big, warm hands knot the handkerchief at the back of her head. A shiver scooted up from her toes and settled like a warm tickle in her belly. His voice moved around to the front of her. Gentle fingertips smoothed down the handkerchief, making sure there were no light leaks.

"Is that comfortable, Lex? Not too tight? And I don't want you worried that we're going to do anything scary. We're just going to walk for a little while and then stop by some water. That's all. Just try to relax and enjoy and inhale the day."

His knuckles brushed her cheek. Then an arm scooped around her shoulder, inviting her to clutch around his waist. There was nothing suggestive about the physical contact, not in his manner or his expression. Cash knew precisely how clumsy she was and was only tucking her securely against his side so she couldn't trip and fall. She got it, she got it. It was just that understanding his practical, prosaic intentions didn't change her response to the situation.

In a slow, easy gait, his hip rocked against hers. And the side of her breast seemed to naturally graze against the side of his ribs. And the warm, strong body under his flannel shirt ignited her senses exactly the way he claimed the exercise was supposed to do—she didn't give a hoot what she could see; she was enjoying her other senses just fine.

Temporarily she didn't care what the Dow Jones was. Or even how her stock portfolio was doing.

"Okay, now, Lex. I want you to ease down to a sitting position. Right now you're standing on a rock—a big one—it's about two-foot square. It's slanted downward and it's rough textured, but there's ample space for you to sit down…and I'll be right next to you. There's water below. You're not going to fall. Just sit. Listen. Smell. Taste."

"Okay." Well…it wasn't precisely okay; she nearly catapulted into the universe when she tried to "ease down." But Cash's hands grabbed her shoulders and steadied her before she'd had time to even think seriously about falling. Then her butt connected with the grainy, damp-cool rock and she sat, like he'd asked. And he sat next to her, like he'd promised.

And although Lexie could have sworn this particular exercise was going reasonably okay so far, suddenly it all went to hell.

It was dark under the blindfold. Obviously. But it wasn't suddenly the scents of pine and earth and the humidity of a sweet-spring rain coming that came to her nostrils. It was the scent of a dark night, from a nightmare ages and ages ago. *Click.* She was three. Huddled in the back of a closet where it was dark and dusty and frightening. She was barefoot, wearing nothing but a nightgown, and she was shivering-cold. *Click.* Someone was in the house. She didn't know who. She just knew that she'd woken up and run into the closet because something was terribly wrong, something making her mom cry out, over and over. And then she heard her daddy's voice, pleading, pleading, desperate. And then an explosion. *Click.*

"Can you hear the waterfall, Lexie? And there are wood violets getting drenched, right at the edge of the woods. And there's a baby squirrel about twenty feet from you. I know you can't see him, but if you concentrate, I'm almost sure you can hear him. He's dancing and prancing all over, full of hell...."

She heard Cash. She heard him. But... *Click.* A nice man in a cop uniform opened the closet door, and he was calling her, lifting her out, using this soothing voice, trying to warm her up. But she understood her mom and daddy were gone forever. She *knew.* And the only thing in her head was this feeling of helplessness and loss. She couldn't stand it. Couldn't stand feeling powerless—not then, not now, not ever. *Click.* She was twenty-eight now, not three. She understood perfectly well that these were flashes of memory, nothing remotely real now, but the darkness of the blindfold seemed to bring it all back. The memories, the feelings of terror and loss, the rage of helplessness...

"Holy cow. Lexie...whoa, whoa, honey..." She felt Cash ripping off the blindfold, felt the cringing blast of daylight in her eyes, saw the panicked look on his face. "What's going on here? You could have taken off the blindfold at any time, didn't you know that? Hell. I never meant to scare you. I had no reason to know anything bothered you like that. You're okay. You're okay, Lexie, you're okay..."

The symptoms were familiar. Same-old, same-old. Her heart tried to thunder out of her chest. Her pulse chugged like a manic jalopy. Her palms went damp and icky-cold, and the stupid frantic feeling seemed to paint her nerves with anxiety. She couldn't breathe, couldn't think, couldn't stop it.

Lexie wanted to give herself a whack upside the head, but right when she was in the middle of one of the dad-blamed anxiety attacks, it was like the weight of a dragon was sitting on her chest.

"I'm okay," she spit out.

"Don't talk, don't talk, just try to calm down—"

"Go away. I'm fine—"

"I'm not going anywhere, you dimwit woman. When you're okay, you're going to tell me what the hell just happened. But right now you just relax or I swear I'll sit on you."

Any other time, she'd have laughed. Not only was he yelling, but he yanked her on his lap, jammed her head against his chest and started patting her back—apparently believing this would comfort her. Except that Cash's big hand was practically slapping her back because he was so agitated...and his heartbeat, which happened to be right next to her ear, was thundering even louder than hers.

Her lungs scooped in air. The sick-panic dread ball in her stomach gradually eased away. The *clicks* stopped.

In the distance, a thin, gurgling waterfall tumbled from a crevice in the hillside, pewter and diamonds, dancing down rocks into a pool of foam below. A black-and-white woodpecker soared past. Squirrels cavorted in and around the pines. Some kind of hairy varmint—a woodchuck?—paused on the other side of the mountain pool to take a sip of the cool, clear water.

She saw it all, but all she felt was her cheek pressed against Cash, her shoulder wedged under his, the heat of his body, the feel of his chin anchoring the top of her head, and yeah...that interesting body part of his, growing, hard and insistently, right where she was sitting on his lap.

When she found her voice, she didn't move. Didn't want to move. But she did try to explain. "For years, I was fine."

"Yeah?"

"My parents were wealthy. Unfortunately wealthy enough to make them an appealing target for thieves. And I was three, almost four, when a burglary went wrong, and both my parents ended up dead. I hid in a closet, which was where the cops found me hours later."

"Hell, Lexie. That's horrible."

"Yeah, it was. Not something anyone could completely forget. But…bad things happen to good people all the time. And I had wonderful folks volunteering to help me from the start. I never spent even a night in foster care. There was no close family—no closer than cousins and an aunt who lived a long distance away—but I had a loving family adopt me from the get-go. They were incredible. They *are* incredible. I love them, they love me—"

"That's all real interesting, but how about if we move to the part about why you freaked out wearing that blindfold?"

"I'm trying to," she assured him. And sighed. "It started about a year ago. Did I tell you that I'm in finance? That I have my own investment firm?"

"Yeah, yeah," he said impatiently, but she had to explain this her own way.

"The thing is, as wonderful as my adoptive family is…I never felt like I fit in. They're blond, I'm brunette. They're tall and athletic and statuesque. I'm a short couch potato. They're always outside doing some active thing. My nose was always in a book. But then I started playing with the stock market when I was fourteen. No big thing, you know? I invested a little birthday money—which was all I had—but I also started keeping records of my picks—"

"Um, Lexie, if you're trying to tell me you're filthy rich, I'm thrilled for you. Really. That's real nice. Only, to be honest, I don't give a damn. Could we move along to how you damn near scared me out of my wits here?''

But the only way she knew how to answer him was to fill in the blanks about her background. "I haven't a clue why I'm lucky with money, Cash. But I am. And the reason it matters is not because I give a hoot about material stuff. It's because, when I was a kid, I struggled so hard to find something I was good at. The money thing gave me an identity, confidence. For the first time since I lost my parents, I started feeling safe and secure. Only then, about a year ago, it stopped.''

"What stopped? The money? You lost some money?''

"No, no. That's just the point. I keep making it. In fact, that's when that ridiculous article came out about me, with that tag about being the Pixie With The Midas Touch. I could have killed 'em. How insulting is that, implying I'm short?''

"Uh, Lexie, I don't think it's slander when somebody's telling the truth—''

"Well, the point is, about a year ago I started getting these anxiety attacks. And insomnia. Really bad. The goofy thing is that I'm still making great money. Nothing's wrong. I'm safer than most people ever get in a lifetime financially. I'm happy, for God's sake. I'm secure. Only suddenly all this stupid money isn't working to make me feel safe. In fact, that's exactly why I came here.''

"Huh?''

"My family are the kind of people who think a few weeks in the wilderness are a cure for anything that ails you. I mean, a few weeks at Silver Mountain are their ideal vacation, not mine. But…in this case I thought they were right. I thought, if I just forced myself to get completely away, I could get a handle on these panic attacks. Get some rest, the strength to emotionally kick myself in the keister. *Make* myself cut it out—or die trying. And it's working, Cash.''

"Wait a minute. I just lost ten years of my life, thinking you were having some kind of heart attack, right here, right now, because of some stupid blindfold I made you wear, and you're telling me it's working?"

He was so upset that she started feeling rattled. She'd never meant to scare Cash or for him to blame himself. Her problems were her problems and had nothing to do with him. And she intended to say just that, but he was on such a rant that she couldn't get a word in. The only thing that never crossed her mind—even for a second—was kissing him.

But somehow she touched his cheek when she was trying to get his attention.

And somehow his mouth was suddenly right there, a pinch away from hers.

And somehow her eyes shot to his at that moment. She saw the way he looked at her. Saw what was in his gaze. And in the next second, all this incredible fabulous hell broke loose.

His mouth tasted warm and male and exotic. Lips teased hers, whispered over hers, then settled down for a generous taste. Tongues touched. Tangoed. Invited the mating dance of another kiss.

A fat, cool raindrop chose that moment to fall out of the sky and splash on her forehead.

The sensation startled her into opening her eyes again for that moment. She saw the streaming pewter waterfall, the green-drenched pines, saw a red-tailed hawk and the fast-moving clouds overhead...but that stuff was just backdrop for Cash. He took up everything that mattered in her focus. His wind-ruffled tawny hair, the sharp lines in his face, the edgy nerves in his eyes...it was those nerves that really jangled her. They were man-nerves. The way he looked at her spoke of tension and hunger and desire.

And then she had to close her eyes again because he took

control of the kiss. Or willingly started his own, and his kiss, holy kamoly, his had the power-punch of a lightning strike.

He leaned her so far back that she had the dizzying sensation of falling, but she seemed to be falling into him, not away. Moments before her pulse had been racing, her heart pounding—both familiar symptoms of another dreaded anxiety attack—yet those same symptoms had entirely different effects now. This was thrilling. Excitement coursed through her pulse, secrets pounding, pounding in her ears, desire clenching between her thighs, and then there was this compelling sensation of need…need as raw as an uncut emerald, bright, sharp, unbearably compelling.

She wanted him.

At twenty-eight, naturally she'd experienced the effect of hormones before, but this didn't seem to be about hormones. This seemed to be about volcanoes. This was: *I don't care about the consequences, take me.* This was: *I don't care I don't care don't stop.* This was…

Belonging.

Or wanting to belong. With him, to him. A big, warm hand smoothed down her throat, parting buttons, sneaking beneath fabric to bare, spare skin. She wore a bra, primarily because she was an idealist and these days there was all that amazing lingerie with hidden wires and cupcakes and padding.

A smile seeped into his kiss. She knew he was smiling, because he kissed her with that smile…just before his thumb flicked open the front latch.

She could have told him it wasn't worth his time. Assuming he could fight his way past all the wire and padding, there was really nothing in there but a couple of bumps.

But oh my. He found those small bumps. And instead of acting as if her smallness bothered him, he acted as if slight-breasted women were the greatest turn-on since Adam first noticed Eve.

Another raindrop splashed on the top of her head. A couple splashed on his, and slivered down his right temple. He didn't seem to notice, and for damn sure, she didn't care. Sooner or later the group would start congregating, looking for their leader. Sooner or later it was going to be lunch. Sooner or later Sammy was going to be home from school. Sooner or later one of them needed to raise a hand and announce this was madness.

She just didn't want it to be her.

She'd never felt safe. Not since losing her parents, not since that nightmare twenty-five years ago. She never seemed to fit in anywhere. Being alone wasn't the worst thing in the universe, but sometimes she felt like a lightning bug, searching the darkness every night for someone of her kind. And it wasn't as if she thought Cash could conceivably be a mate...but right then, right *then,* he felt precious. She felt connected to him like she'd only dreamed of connecting to someone else. He bared his loneliness as honestly as she did; chemistry seemed to be exploding for both of them the same way...

"Lex..."

"What?"

"It's pouring."

"So?" She touched his cheek, his jaw. She'd been lucky in her life. She knew that. But not so lucky that she'd ever felt this kind of wonder...and okay, okay, the lust was a wallop of power as well. But this feeling of rightness was so unexpected. Whether it was madness or not, she felt as if she and Cash were discovering something few people ever did. She felt immersed in the emotion of a special man, as if she were on the brink of something huge, a magical cliff, a change that could affect her whole life.

"Lex..." His eyes were closed, and tried opening again. He seemed to be attempting to conjure up a mean expression. "There's *thunder.*"

"Oh. Yeah. You think we should get around to moving, huh?"

"Did you have in mind making love on these rocks in a lightning storm?"

She had to smile. The rain was quickly soaking both of them. It had already painted his hair with a glisten and beaded on his eyelashes. Yet still he kissed her, once more, a long, slow, lazy kiss that in spite of both their bad intentions was eventually interrupted by just-plain discomfort.

"McKay..."

"What?"

"It's pouring."

"For Pete's sake, that's what I tried to tell you. An hour ago."

"It didn't matter then. But now...I'm awfully wet."

"I know."

"McKay. Not *that* kind of wet. Could you try to get your mind off sex and onto something constructive? Like rescuing me and the rest of the guests?"

"Me? You think *my* mind's on sex—?"

"I know it is," she said in her best prim-proper voice— as she buttoned up her shirt, and then his. When she pushed off his lap and lurched to her feet, though, nothing seemed normal. The whole world was loopy, unsteady, and the cold, damp rain was shiver-soaking down her spine now. "Next time, for heaven's sake, don't start something unless we're under cover, someplace warm and dry," she said severely.

Cash sputtered out some kind of response in between a bark of a laugh. She peeled ahead of him, well aware that the rest of the guys had to be either hightailing it for the lodge and racing through the rain, seeking Cash. Either way she didn't want him caught in an intimate clutch with her, for his sake.

She wasn't sure what had just happened between them. Her nerves were still singing, her heart still soaring...and need still crying in her hormones as well. She had an outstanding excuse. No other man had ever made her feel this way.

But Cash had already made it diamond-clear that Sammy was his priority. Meaning he got involved with no women, and especially not city women who had no chance of staying in their lives.

The light teasing she'd tried wasn't really what her heart was feeling...but his bark of a laugh had reassured her. Playing this light with him was best.

She wouldn't want Cash thinking any damn fool petrifying thing—like that she was falling in love with him.

This whole day just kept getting more and more uncomfortable. Quieter than a sneak, Lexie tiptoed from the women's showers to the door of the masseur's room, with a towel clamped under her arms in a vise grip. She made it as far as touching the doorknob before she stalled.

Outside the gym facility, thunder boomed. Rain shot the windows with silver bullets. Instead of the normal bright light of a late spring afternoon, the sky was darker than pitch—only meaner and gloomier.

A few minutes earlier, getting a massage had seemed a terrific idea. She'd been unnerved and tense ever since almost making love to Cash that morning. Apparently he was, too, because he'd assembled the group and made 'em hike in the rain for a merciless couple of hours, claiming they'd get into it, that the smells and tastes and sounds in the rain were an experience they'd enjoy if they just let it happen.

Yeah, right. More like the two of them had both been trying to outrun a dragon on their tail. To give herself credit, she'd actually managed to keep up with the guys on that long hike. Only now, she was chilled, whipped, bruised and cranky. The lodge services included a massage room, and she figured this afternoon was a perfect time to indulge.

Just a wee bit late, though, she remembered that she didn't "do" masseurs. Ever. She had enough trouble getting naked with men she knew. Men she didn't know were out of the question. Other women were fabulously assertive, comfortable with their bodies and happy to stand up for what they enjoyed. And then, Lexie thought, there were the mice of the world. Like her. Women who never owned a bikini and wore turtlenecks on dates and clutched up at the thought of exposing anything as wild as a thigh in front of a stranger.

Of course, she'd nearly exposed a lot more than a thigh in front of Cash this morning. Remembering seemed to shock her spine into stiffening, and she pushed open the masseur's door.

Almost the instant she stepped inside, her worry level diminished. There was nothing to fret here. The small, white room smelled like soap and baby oil. The temperature was warm, the furnishings limited to a white cabinet and supply cart and a single, long stretcher cot. Nothing in the setup looked remotely frightening—except for the behemoth of a giant who suddenly loped around a corner, snapping a towel in his wake. "You have to be Lexie. Hey, come on in. I was wondering when you were going to get around to chasing me down, and you picked a great time, because I've got the next hour free. I'm Bubba."

"Bubba," she echoed, even though the whole world had already told her the masseur's name. She just hadn't anticipated it would fit him so well.

"Well, the real name's Murphy, but nobody's called me anything but Bubba for as long as I can remember. And it seems everybody's wanting a rubdown today. It's the storm, I think. Makes y'all tense and edgy."

"Um, I'm not exactly sure—"

He only had to glance at her face once. "Trust me, there's nothing to sweat. I'm gay. Besides which, you don't have to uncover anything you want to stay covered. I started out in physical therapy, been doing this for years. To start with, I'll give you a choice of oils…and then you tell me if you have any special sore spots. Then you just come on up on the table and lay down on your stomach, and we'll get started, see how it goes for you, okay?''

Gay, her mind echoed, as her gaze roamed the six-foot-two chunky beefcake with the oiled muscles and the door-sized feet. ''Um, I just haven't done anything like this before—''

''Hey, ain't you seen the hair color commercial? Aren't you worth it? Hasn't Cash been running your tush off?''

''Yes, he has,'' she said feelingly.

''And Keegan, he's been making you eat that god-awful granola.''

''Yes, he has,'' she repeated.

''And George now…our housekeeper's such a grump that he probably tore your head off if you even tried talking to him—''

''He was nice, actually. But you're right, he does tend to be a little testy.''

''See? Just like that other old commercial goes—you deserve a break today.'' He thumped the stretcher cot. ''Just come on up here. I'll make you feel better. I promise.''

Gay, she mentally reminded herself. Safe. ''Okay,'' she said, and leaped onto the table…nearly upsetting his cartful of oils.

Her clumsiness neither bothered nor slowed down Bubba. Within seconds he'd attacked. With hands as big as bread loaves, he started pummeling. Molding. Kneading. ''Gee willickers, you're tense to beat the band, babe. You really are a mess.''

''Thanks so much.''

He grinned. ''Don't worry about it. I can fix you up.''

Possibly he could, Lexie mused, but she considered it more likely that he'd kill her before he cured her. Momentarily, though, a tiny whoosh of cool air made her realize that someone had opened the door. And then she heard a familiar voice. "How's it going, Lexie?"

Sammy. Company. Someone human to talk to, who wasn't a grown-up testosterone machine. She checked to make sure she wasn't going to embarrass him, or himself, but the only body part Bubba had exposed were her shoulders. "Just great, Sammy. And I was just thinking that you had to be getting home from school around now."

"Yeah, it was stupid to go at all. We're not doing anything. Great storm, huh?" He climbed on the cabinet top near her head, swinging his legs amiably. "Bubba rubs me down sometimes, too."

"Does he?"

"Are you sore, Lexie?"

"I was. A little. When I first came in."

"Yeah, well, most of you city guys are flabby when you first come here. That's why Cash and me do these programs. You couldn't last a day in the woods alone. But it still takes a while to build up. You can't just get muscles overnight. And you're a girl besides, so you're a lot weaker."

"Are you trying to get yourself killed, young man?" Lexie used her most threatening voice, but Sammy only giggled delightedly. He already had teasing her down to a science. "I haven't seen Martha all day. How's she doing?"

"She's still pregnant." He sighed. "She just keeps getting bigger and bigger, but she never has the puppies. Well, I gotta go." He slid down from the cabinet and gave her an innocent look. "I'm gonna go have some cookies, turn on the tube, listen to some Down Jones…"

"Down Jo—Sammy, you come back here, you tease—"

Sammy was chortling hard as he closed the door behind him. She'd just closed her eyes and settled down to suffer Bubba's administrations again when the door whooshed open a second time.

"Hey, Bubba, how are Trixie and the kids?"

When Lexie heard Cash's voice, her head bolted upright faster than a jack-in-the-box. And never mind if she was towel-draped from stem to stern, she suddenly felt more naked than a newborn—only a grown-up, female version of a newborn. She also heard Cash referring to Bubba's wife and kids, and Bubba's lazy, easy reply. "Just fine, just fine. Max, he's growing like a weed, into trouble all the time. And Cinderella, well, we're still potty-training. I think we're gonna be potty-training that one when she's fifty."

"Whatever happened to 'gay'?" Lexie wondered aloud.

Bubba's beefy hand pushed her head down to that flat pillow again. "Made you quit feeling nervous around me, didn't it?"

Cash, his voice amused, provided a little further information. "Bubba was a physical therapist, back when he lived in civilization and thought he wanted to live a real life."

"Yeah, but then I made the mistake of getting married and having two kids. My days of hunting and fishing are a distant memory. Damn lucky I wasn't stuck bringing one of the kids with me—hell, this muscle in your calf's knotted up enough to charley horse on you. Quit talking and relax, Lexie, or I'm gonna have to get tough."

Relax? She'd almost *been* relaxed when Sammy was here, and Bubba—gay or not gay—had stopped being any kind of worry. But Cash was a different story.

He'd driven himself harder than anyone else that day, but it sure didn't show. He leaned against the same cabinet that his son had chosen to perch on, and lazily cocked a boot forward. His hair was still shaggy with rain, his boots damp, his jeans hugging his long lean frame, his gaze full of…energy. Vital, virile, sexy male energy. And he'd chosen a natural enough place to be able to talk to her, look at her.

But didn't anyone ever hear of privacy around here? Modesty? Peace?

"I didn't figure I'd catch up with you until dinner, and by then, everybody'll be there. I just wanted to see you for a second, make sure you were okay."

She wasn't sure if he meant okay, recovered from her anxiety attack. Or okay, recovered from his kisses. "Yes and no," she said cautiously, disbelieving he was trying to talk to her in front of Bubba.

"She's knotted up like a lariat," Bubba complained. "Gonna have to work like a dog to get her right again. Don't be letting her do anything big tomorrow. She's too much of a tenderfoot."

"Tenderfoot? Excuse me? I'm tougher than nails," she assured them both.

"Sammy came in to check on her earlier," Bubba informed Cash, as if she hadn't spoken. "Whispered to me to take care of her, like he was her hundred-year-old bodyguard. Pretty obvious he's crazy for her. Think he said he was going off to get some cookies and sack out in front of the boob tube."

Cash pushed away from the counter. "Well, I'd better catch up with him." A fingertip stroked her bare shoulder. Not an exotic touch. Not a sexy touch. But hormones bolted straight to her nerves from that simple, familiar contact. "Lexie, after Sammy's tucked in tonight, could I have a few minutes to talk to you?"

"Sure," she said, but the request put a gulp in her throat. One tête-à-tête with Cash a day was proving more than she could handle. Two was double-worrisome. And what could he possibly want to talk to her about, that they hadn't already said to each other earlier?

Six

The minute Cash tucked Sammy in, he charged into the living room. The place needed some rearranging as well as a classic 52-Pick-Up, and he'd taken so much time putting the squirt to bed that Lexie was really already overdue. Swiftly he tuned on CNBC, folded a fresh *Wall Street Journal* on the coffee table, switched on Sammy's computer in the corner and then located a traveling phone within arm's reach of the couch. After that, he stood back, studying, wanting all the seductive technology in Lexie's eyesight the instant she strolled in.

By the time he heard the quiet rap on the door, he jogged to answer it, telling himself that he was ready—and then mentally laughed at the lies a guy could tell himself.

He was never ready. Not for Lexie. A guy would have to brace himself with emotional steel girders to be ready for Lexie.

Because he'd known she was coming, he'd put on clean

jeans and a black T-shirt with no holes and socks. Typically, though, her version of dressing for a crash-at-home evening was attire more suited to an urban shindig. The marled cotton sweater was done in muted sunset hues; the swishy-fabric slacks weren't pink or coral or peach or anything exactly, but one of those pale shades in-between. Her sandals matched that impossible shade precisely, so did her dangling earrings and hint of cheek blush.

His version of "casual" would never be hers, but Cash had long figured out that clothes were a front-line defense for Lexie. There was no question that she liked her girl-clothes, but the more carefully she put herself together, the more he realized she tended to be extra worried about something.

And he saw the clothes…but what he really noticed was the sweet curve of her rump and the way she'd pushed her hair behind her ears tonight. He could have sworn he'd carefully prepared this whole encounter with her, but his plans suddenly fizzled like smoke. In his mind, he saw her from this afternoon, when Bubba's hands were working on the tight muscles in her neck. That long, white towel had modestly covered her entire length, but her fanny had still been sticking up, the long, long slope of her spine an uphill road for his eyes, and her naked shoulders something he could have visually feasted on until the cows came home—or later. The more Bubba pummeled and beat out those tension knots, the sleepier and sexier her eyes became. And then he'd noticed the oil on her skin. Slippery. Silky. Fragrant. Making him think how she'd look sweaty during sex…with him. Because he sure as hell wanted to get sweaty, specifically with her.

Hell. This little meeting was never going to work, no matter how much he'd conned himself into believing it was an inspired idea.

"Is Sammy asleep?" she whispered as she stepped in.

"By a miracle, yes. He's not always a good sleeper, but tonight he conked out like a bugler playing 'Taps.' Come on in, sit down..." Sheesh. He hadn't even noticed the soccer ball on the couch before, but now he hustled to shoot it behind a chair out of sight. "Would you like a glass of wine? Say yes."

"Why?" she asked wryly.

"Because Keegan told me to offer you wine instead of beer, so I've got both red and white that'll live forever in my refrigerator if you don't want any."

"In that case, more than anything on earth, I'd desperately like a glass of red wine."

"Thank God." He galloped into his mini kitchen area, battled the cork, filched a glass and poured in the burgundy. When he hustled back in, he expected to find her zombie-eyed and near orgasm in front of the Dow Jones scores for the day, but she wasn't even looking at CNBC. She was still standing, waiting for him. She blinked at the size of glass he handed her, and then motioned around the room as if she'd been studying it for quite a while. "Don't tell me two guys live here."

"Shocked, huh? Was the soccer ball the giveaway?"

"Oh, it wasn't any one thing...more like a combination of the soccer ball, the boat anchor on the table, the back-packs, the socks, the jackets being used as couch pillows, the no-drapes, the—"

"Hey. We got rid of the lamp that was shaped like a naked woman. It's not like we're not trying to become more civilized. Sip up," he urged her.

She sipped. Like a girl. "But what's really blowing me away is your allowing me into the private sanctum. And you have the TV on. Somehow I wouldn't guess that you'd normally be all that riveted by the business news channel."

"If you're asking if I turned it on just for you—you're damn right." When she finally settled on the couch, he hunkered down in the chair across from her, his expression turning serious. "I wanted you to get a look at the market numbers. And see any other financial stuff you wanted. That anxiety attack you had this morning shook the starch out of me, Lex. This was never supposed to be an army boot camp. Taking your electronic stuff away was just camp rules, to coax you to give the fresh air and wilderness experience a chance. It wasn't supposed to upset you. It was supposed to help. But if you want access to all that stuff again, fine. I don't want you having any more anxiety attacks."

She hesitated, her eyes meeting his over the wineglass. "Is that why you asked to talk to me tonight?"

"Yeah. That, and a little change in the program. Listen, Lex." He hunched forward, elbows on his knees, like a football coach. "I didn't know about those panic attacks of yours before. And I'm no psychologist, nor do I want to be. But nobody leaves Silver Mountain who isn't in better shape than when they came. That's the rule."

She nodded sagely. "It's a matter of pride."

"Right. *My* pride." He thought, so far, this was going real good. She *did* have a great sense of humor, and he felt relieved she didn't know how carefully he wasn't talking about sex. Or kisses. Or them. "See, my pride is directly connected to my business. You have to be *happy* when you leave this place. That's how I build my reputation. Happy clients. And the problem is that I'm no great businessman, nor ever wanted to be. But this is Sammy's financial future, so I have to make this place work. And that means, you can't have any more panic attacks, and that's that. Furthermore, we have to find some way for you to have a terrific time from now on. So. I'm thinking tomorrow, we'll try sailing."

She raised her eyebrows. "I think I understood most of your lecture there. Unless I'm happy, I could jeopardize your son's entire financial future, was that the message?"

"Uh-huh."

She gave a deadpan nod. "Okay. I'm happy now. But I'll be even happier from now on. We can't have Sammy's entire future jeopardized, now can we? But the part I didn't understand was about the sailing. Like, what's new? I thought sailing was already automatically part of the program."

"It is, it is. In fact, there's a little mountain lake at the far south end of the property, just big enough to have some fun in a Hobie Cat. But the point is…from now on, I don't want any more outside activity adding to your stress. We do most of our programs hands-on. But not for you. Not anymore. We'll still go out on the water tomorrow, but I'll do the actual sailing, the work. And you're going to do the relaxing. You're—"

"Cash," she interrupted.

"What?" Clearly she'd been having fun with him until that point, but now her gaze met his and her voice turned soft-quiet.

"Do you think I have a mental screw loose, because of having those panic attacks?"

"Hell no. Everybody has stuff that spooks 'em. And that was one big terrifying trauma you survived as a kid, hiding in a dark closet when that burglary and murder was going on. I thought about it this afternoon. How I'd get the willies same way, wouldn't like it if anyone blinded my eyes or I felt cooped up in a dark place."

"Uh-huh. Sure you would." She tilted her head, as if she'd happened to notice how industriously he was refolding the newspaper and she was determined to force a little direct eye-to-eye contact. "Let's try a question a little more to the point. This morning, did you think I came onto you because I was having an anxiety attack? Not in my right mind? Not thinking clearly?"

Cripes, they'd been doing so well. He'd planned all this

stuff to say to her, specifically so her mind would be completely diverted from that accidental explosion of chemistry and the accidental explosion before that. Swiftly Cash grabbed the remote control and started pushing the trigger. "Hey, if CNBC isn't your favorite channel, let's find you some other kind of financial news. There's all kind of money stuff I can get you on the satellite. You just sip a little wine, put your feet up...wow. Is the hog market down or what?"

"Do you follow the hog market, McKay?"

"Not exactly."

"Pigs aren't my cup of tea, either." Gently she removed the remote control from his hand, and clicked off the TV altogether. "I wasn't off my tree. I knew what I was doing when I kissed you back. That doesn't mean we have to invite that kind of trouble again. But I don't want you thinking that I must have been having a mental breakdown to enjoy kissing you. I loved every moment. Thoroughly."

"Okeydoke. That's real clear," he said heartily. "Maybe you'd like to watch CNBC now?"

"No." Her slim, white hand reached over...and just touched his. As soft as the soothing stroke of silk on a burn. "I don't quite understand how these clinch things keep happening between us or what we should do about it. But I already know I couldn't possibly fit in your life here. I already know that it'd be upsetting for Sammy to have another woman in his life take off on him. So stop worrying, Cash. No matter what happens between you and me, I won't be making anything awkward for you, and that's a promise. Now, how about if you tell me about Sammy's mom?"

"You want to know about Hannah?" And yeah, he'd heard her. It was just that she was taking him out, being so up-front and honest. It also bugged him, that she was so sure she didn't fit in. And no, damnation, of course she didn't. They were chalk and cheese in their choice of lifestyles. He should have felt relieved she was so blunt and open.

Instead he felt aggravated. He was the guy. He should be protecting her against potential hurt, and instead the darn woman always seemed to sound like she was looking out for him.

"Yes, I'd like to know more about Hannah," she affirmed. "At least, I thought that's what you said your sister's name was. Hannah is Sammy's mother, right?"

"Yeah." Abruptly Cash wished he were more of a drinking man. A couple double shots of whiskey would go down easy about now. His pulse was kicking hard, his nerves itchy. It just wasn't a good idea, his liking her so much. The lust thing wasn't that troublesome. A good old powerful lust attack was a lot of fun. But he just plain *liked* Lexie. Enjoyed being with her. Respected her honesty and her humor and her sharpness. And if that problem weren't tough enough, the damn woman had to bring up his sister. He never felt comfortable talking about Hannah.

"Quit looking at the hallway, Cash. I'll tell you if Sammy shows up in the doorway. I don't want him hearing anything he shouldn't, either. But I see him every day. I'm crazy about him, and I don't want to do or say anything wrong to him if I can avoid it. It'd help if I understood what the situation with his mother is."

"Yeah, I agree, and I don't mind your knowing. I just don't know what to say. I never know what to say about Hannah." He gestured vaguely. "She and my mother were two peas in a pod. Dreamers. I swear both of them believed in Prince Charming, that in a good life, a man took care of the woman completely, treated her like a princess."

"And where did they get that idea?"

Hell. Did she *have* to hone on in the sore spot in the story? "Well, it's possible they got some of those ideas from the men in the family. The guys were all brought up with the old code of honor. It's a man's job to take care of a woman. Women are meant to be pampered and protected. That kind of thing. When I was a kid, I thought my dad really valued women. But when I grew up, and saw how Hannah turned out…well, it seems like what my dad was really doing was unconsciously putting her down, and my mother, too. Like he'd buy my mom presents and flowers and trinkets up the wazoo, which made him look like a good guy who was spoiling her?—except that whenever he wanted to do something, he just did it. He was an autocrat. She never had to work, but she never got a vote in how they lived, either.''

''And that was what your sister wanted out of life, too?''

Cash lifted both his hands. ''Everything I can say makes her sound bad. Selfish. Coldhearted. But it's not that simple.'' He sighed. ''You'd love her if you met her. Everyone always did. She's funny and entertaining and sweet. If she thought you were cold, she'd give you the shirt off her back. But when she got pregnant…I don't know, it all just crashed in on her. She was counting on the guy to marry her, take care of her. And when the baby was finally born, it hit her like a bullet that this was a twenty-four-hour-a-day job. She just couldn't seem to handle the responsibility. She took off.''

''So she left when Sammy was a baby,'' Lexie probed gently. ''But that was a long time ago. Why hasn't she come back? Or taken him with her?''

''Damned if I know. I think in the beginning, she felt ashamed. Too ashamed to come home. Only then, the longer she stayed away, the tougher it got for her to believe she could come back and make it up, especially to Sammy. So she quit trying. She calls once in a while, and hell…'' He scraped a hand through his hair. ''I yelled at her a couple of times. That didn't help. I *know* that now, but what was I supposed to do? Make out like it was okay she was behaving like an irresponsible turkey? It's not okay, damn it. And even though Sammy seems fine most of the time, I can see he's got his own special little problems that obviously stem from—''

''He told me about wetting the bed.''

Cash's jaw dropped. ''You're kidding? He told you about that? He *never* tells anyone.'' And yet, with that secret out of the bag, he couldn't see a purpose in hiding another. ''The kid thinks there's something wrong with him. Always has. For all I know, he always will. He got this idea that his mom would never have taken off if she loved him—ergo, there must be something unlovable about him.''

''Oh, Cash, I know.''

''You don't…'' He snicked off that thought. ''Yeah, you probably do know, don't you?''

''Well, I never had to doubt that I was loved, the way Sammy's mother has made him feel. But I think there's something that happens when any child is orphaned. They tend to feel a little misplaced, like the toy that won't fit in the box, or a piece that doesn't go in anybody else's puzzle. You just never feel the same sense of security that kids in a regular family feel. Nothing turned things around in my life until I started making money.''

''Money?''

She nodded. ''I know I told you about this before. It wasn't the riches that mattered, but discovering that I had a talent, something of my *own*.'' She'd long since put down the huge glass of wine and snugged her arms under her chest. ''The reason I'm mentioning it again is so that you know, that's the kind of thing that Sammy and I talk about. What he loves doing. The kinds of things that make him feel good. I've been trying to help him identify the special gifts he has, you know? Just to give him the idea that the sense of security that matters comes from the inside, from how you feel about yourself. You get me?''

''Sure,'' Cash said, but that was a lie. He was listening. And her compassion and understanding for Sammy—a kid she barely knew, for Pete's sake—were touching him, and he wasn't a man who thought of himself as "touchable." But it was watching her that was blowing him away. Man, she had so much love in her. She was all roiled up, like a busty spring wind, exuberant, happy. Here she was just talking about Sammy, yet caring brought out the passion in her voice, the fire in her eyes.

"You know what one of your special gifts is, McKay? You've got a Midas Touch with people."

"Huh? I could never hold onto a dime unless it was taped in my wallet."

"I'm not talking about coins and bills. I'm saying that you have heart to burn. All these strangers come here, invariably stressed out, festering something on the inside. You ferret out whatever it is, give them things to do that give the spirit a chance to ease and heal. Like the exercise this morning, when everyone was blindfolded. Later, it occurred to me how that worked. You had to trust the other person— and I suspect most executives have a hard time trusting their staff or anyone else. They don't feel safe when they give up control. So that was an extra helpful type of exercise—"

"Not too helpful. It didn't work worth beans for you."

"No, but that's just because I'm goofy and have an old nightmare." She grinned, and then suddenly popped to her feet. "Well, I'd better be heading upstairs. The taskmaster around here is so tough that we all have to get up early. And you're all straightened out, right?"

"Me? Straightened out?"

"Uh-huh." A little wine sloshed out of her glass when her knee bumped it. Straightening that, she unsettled a stack of magazines—sending a couple shimmying to the floor. He grabbed the rest the same as she did. "You're not still worried that I'm going to make a big deal out of those kisses, are you? We're all set."

"All set?" he echoed, feeling like a moronic mimic, but

not expecting her to take this conversational track in any way. Or for her to smile at him with such lazy, easy mischief.

"That's why you really invited me to stop by, wasn't it? To make sure I wasn't going to make a federal case out of a kiss here and there. Or to presume we have some kind of 'relationship' because a few hormones kick up when we're together."

The magazines were all lined up again and Lexie aimed for the door before he could think of anything to respond. The last Cash knew, he'd invited her to stop by so they could work out a more amenable program for her. Make sure she was okay after that anxiety attack. And yeah, he'd been a little nervous what she was making of that clinch this morning. Still, Lexie was never supposed to know—or guess—that what she called "a few hormones" had damn near given him a heart attack. And then some. And now for some reason his blood pressure was trying to simmer all over again.

"You thought I was *worried?*" he repeated.

"It's understandable. You have Sammy. I know you're already concerned that Sammy could get attached to another woman who doesn't stick around, but I'm guessing you've had other touchy situations to deal with besides that. You cater to a fairly wealthy clientele here, so I'll bet you've had more than one woman check in, decide she likes your program as well as Silver Mountain's—and just presume she can take what she sees. Right? Aw, Cash, I hope I'm not making you uncomfortable talking about this. All I'm trying to say is that you don't need to worry. I definitely wasn't expecting that click between us, but you can take it to the bank, I won't do anything to hurt Sammy. And God knows, you don't have to worry about my pushing myself on you. I'm well aware that I don't belong here. And a couple of weeks from now, I'll be gone, out of your hair."

When she promptly hightailed it for the door, he galloped

after her, intending to open it. To say good-night. To get rid of her. The more she'd talked in that patient, careful voice, the more something got messed up in his head.

He had no idea why he wanted to punch the nearest wall. Why his blood pressure was past simmer and had moved onto a rollicking boil. Why he was ticked enough to chew nails. She was being nice, for God's sake. Making sure he wasn't worried there was, or could be, anything between them. She was a bachelor's dream. His personal ideal fantasy. Everything was hunky-dory about the whole short little encounter.

But when he yanked open the door to let her out, he accidentally seemed to slam it closed again. And then he accidentally seemed to swoop down, scowling at her like a cranky ogre—feeling meaner than a cranky ogre, too. Only then he seemed to accidentally kiss her.

And when the damn woman was pushed up against the wall, having the smile kissed right off her—and then some—instead of socking him...the way any intelligent woman would have...her fingertips climbed up his arms and slowly, slowly ribboned around his neck.

A mean kiss suddenly turned misty.

A mad mood suddenly turned manic.

A macho pass suddenly had a complete shift of power, and became her kiss instead of his. Her taking out a mood on him, instead of the other way around. His knees were knocking. His hands unsteady. His lungs begging for oxygen in gulps...when it was supposed to be her, bowled over by his experienced sexual prowess.

The damn woman didn't *have* any prowess.

But man. Could she kiss. Lexie could make a man believe he was the hottest thing to ever emerge from a *y* chromosome. The only guy in her universe. The only man she ever needed or ever wanted in her universe. The only man...

Aw, hell. Whatever she did to him, he didn't understand

and couldn't explain—but it was better than anything he could remember feeling. If she was a drug, then he wanted the addiction. If she was bad news, he wanted all the graphic details. If she was his worst fear, who cared? He'd had no conception before that terror could be this much fun.

Her breasts cuddled flat and evocatively against his chest. Her pelvis rocked against his, igniting hormones that had been nicely sleeping for him for years. Need bayed through him like a lonesome hound. Desire clutched in his head and fastened on, desire that had her name, her scent, the very specific shape of her soft, red mouth. And he'd had enough of her clothes to last a lifetime. He wanted her naked and beneath him. Now. Yesterday. Enough of this messing around. He was losing his mind. For her. In her. With her. And for Pete's sake, he didn't even have her sweater off.

In that precise second, though, he had to pull back from a kiss because of the drastic shortage of oxygen. Annoying as it was, his lungs still seemed to think air was a necessity. Not like he wanted to let her go, even for a second, but once he'd pulled back…well. It seemed her eyes were open. Waiting for him.

Huge eyes.

Vulnerable eyes.

Her mouth was still red from the pressure of his kisses, a spot on her throat whisker-burned, and the willingness in those eyes took him out and then some. "You're not still mad at me, are you?" she whispered.

"Mad? I was never mad. And for damn sure, I was never mad at you."

"Uh-huh." She nodded with one of those knowing woman-smiles. "It'd help if you gave me a little warning if you got mad the next time, okay?"

"I wasn't mad."

"Okay." Another smile, this one silky. Soft. So were the fingertips on his cheek. "G'night, sweetie."

Sweetie? Him? No woman on the planet had ever called him ''sweetie'' for the obvious reason that he wasn't. And just like that she was gone, out the door, headed up the lodge stairs, leaving him standing in the doorway in physical and mental shambles.

He let out a sigh that was like the hiss of steam released from a pressure cooker. He wasn't in love with her. Even if he *wanted* to be in love with her, he couldn't get attached to a woman who wouldn't stay, for Sammy's sake. That was it. Cut-and-dried. No excuses, no exceptions. And women had always been the bane of his life—he *knew* that—so Lexie wasn't even an exception in that sense.

But man, she sure had him churned up all ways from Sunday. Nothing wrong with a buzz. Nothing wrong with a hot affair. Nothing wrong with two consenting adults making a choice to enjoy something together, only dad-nabbit, he knew damn well nothing would be simple with her.

She didn't kiss like the kiss was play.

She kissed for keeps.

She kissed like it mattered.

And damned if Cash had a clue what to do about it. But by tomorrow, when he took her sailing, he had to figure it out.

Seven

Lexie pushed her hands into her back pockets, trying not to shiver, staring at the lake, waiting for Cash. He'd warned her that he couldn't be here before ten. He had the usual group to get started on the morning's exercise, she knew. And he wasn't the least late for their sailing date—she was early.

It was hard to look forward to sailing, when Lexie was absolutely sure that she was either going to tip them over or cause some other disaster, but still she'd been up at five, anticipating this time with him. And she'd dressed with meticulous care to win herself some confidence—white duck pants, white boat-necked top, navy-blue light jacket with an anchor on the sleeve…and, of course, Sammy's incongruously old battered tennis shoes. The shoes went with nothing, but she didn't care. Sammy's shoes had become a good luck symbol. She'd never been trying to win a fashion contest—people around here couldn't care less how she dressed.

But clothes were like a rabbit's foot for her. If she was wearing the wrong thing, something would go wrong. Guys never got that, but any woman on the planet would understand.

She stopped pacing the lakeshore long enough to chew on a thumbnail. Memories from last night whiskered through her mind. Again. Cash had given her every chance to see the ticker tape, get on the Internet, send a fax. She hadn't even peeked at CNBC.

Something was badly wrong with her. And getting worse. Thinking money—doing money—had always made her feel safe. It was the only thing she was great at. The one thing that always made the emotional dragons go back into the closet. It was the unique thing that was hers, that made her feel strong and powerful.

Only right now she felt as powerful as a butterfly. Abruptly she slugged her hands back into her pockets. She couldn't keep her mind on money. She no longer gave a damn about clothes. Her whole familiar world seemed to be falling apart. Her new and uncomfortable reality was that she only had eyes for Cash, loping through the trees, sauntering down to the dock edge.

Toward her.

She started tapping her foot. Damn man looked like a young Indiana Jones. Crooked smile. Eyes full of hell and sex appeal. Giving off testosterone from fifty yards away, and no guy should be able to look that good in old, battered jeans and a worn-out Henley.

His appeal was getting downright exasperating.

Behind her, the lake slip-slopped on the stony shore—although personally, Lexie thought calling it a lake was a mighty exaggeration. A wildly overgrown pond was more like it.

She liked the spot, she had to admit that much. The stony edge had piles of jewels in it—garnets and gold and veins of Lapis—and if those stones weren't really gems, only Ma Nature and a jeweler could know the difference. On sunny days the water gleamed like silver. Not today. This morning, dirty clouds scuttled across the sky, pushed by a fretful wind, dulling the water color to a dusty pewter.

Leaves hissed in the spring breeze, a breeze that she supposed made this technically a good sailing day. But the boat looked more like something a child would put in a bathtub than a real boat to her. The sail was adorable, striped in rainbow colors, but if two people were going to sit in the sucker, they were certain to be snuggling hip to hip.

Not that she minded being hip to hip with Cash, exactly. Fantasies of making love with him had been dominating her dreams—which was another new thing in her life that the blasted man had affected. Sleeping. She hadn't done it so long that she'd forgotten what it was like to sleep, much less dream. But she'd been forced into this confounding, exhausting physical schedule for two weeks now, and it was starting to take its toll. The slave driver—alias Cash—never called a halt until everyone was whipped, and then the blasted man made sure no one got any coffee or chocolate after dinner. You'd think he was dealing with children, for pity's sake.

But the worst part about finally getting a real night's sleep was that she'd started dreaming.

Specifically she'd started dreaming about him. Long, lanky and naked. Laughing and naked. Scowling and naked. Any way you cut the dreams, he was usually running around bare-rumped with his personal rascal kidnapping her attention. Invariably in the dream, he was motioning for her to come toward him, and in the shadows just behind him, she always caught sight of a king-size bed. Other details smudged in her mind, but through the blur she remembered a feather mattress. Candles smelling like peaches and vanilla. The sound of water from somewhere—not dripping water, but the soothing, enticing gurgling of a stream. But forgetting the water, the scents, the night shadows—the one consistent thing in the dreams was that Cash was never in the shadows, but only in the light. And he kept motioning toward her, wanting her to come to him.

For sex, she'd told herself in the dream.

And she was starting to think, just maybe, that sex was a good idea for real. In part, she'd understood her attraction for Cash from the get-go. He was rock solid, a special man who stood by those he loved, who came with an extra dollop of both heart and soul and never backed down from an unusual course. Falling in love with the guy was easy. It was the sex thing that was getting…upsetting.

She was getting tired of wanting Cash. Tired of feeling lightning bolts in the air whenever he ambled into a room. Tired of feeling her hormones sizzle and her body parts snap awake, only to feel frustrated when there was no resolution in sight. Sleeping with him would cure that ailment, she thought. If she'd just *do* it and get it over with, Lexie was almost positive she could get her real life back in order again. She'd done sex before. It was no big deal. It was the worrying about it and thinking about it with *him* that had somehow become a blasted big deal. The frustration had become like a sliver festering between them.

He didn't want her around long-term. She'd known that from day one. And that was fine, not a source of hurt in any way. So she didn't fit into his life. So what? She'd never belonged anywhere. She'd grown up, quit baying at that moon, quit yearning for the stars she couldn't have. But what was wrong with loving him, as long as she didn't hurt him or Sammy?

The devil had finally ambled the rest of the way down the hillside and reached her side. He cocked a lazy foot forward, but not until he was close enough that she could see the tip of his grin and the bad-boy gleam in his eyes. "Hey, shorty."

"Don't you call me shorty, cowboy."

The loping, lazy grin intensified. "Hard to call you anything else. Sammy's going to be taller than you—and probably by next week. But I forgot. I didn't mean to tease you this early in the morning. By now you'd think I'd remember that you wake up testier than a hungry porcupine."

At that insult, she brushed a flicker of lint from her spotless white duck pants. "And you wake up so perky that it's no wonder you have to live in the wilderness. Somebody'd kill you if you pulled this cheerful routine at this hour of the morning anywhere civilized."

"You call places like Chicago and New York and L.A. civilized? Last I noticed, cities were jungles."

"The point," she said darkly, "is your being so incessantly *nice* in the morning."

"All right, all right, I admit it's a problem. In fact, to tell the truth, living in the wilderness is no protection. People have tried killing me here, too. But in the meantime, did you get a look at our fourteen-foot Hobie? Isn't she a beauty? You're gonna love sailing, trust me."

Another look at the boat was enough to sober a drunk, and Lexie hadn't even had coffee. "Listen, McKay, before we go anywhere near that toy, I need to ask you a serious question. Can I tip it over?"

"Nope."

"I mean it. I'm worried. You know how clumsy I am—"

He bent down and unzipped a gear bag. God knew Cash never went anywhere without a gear bag. Women traveled with purses, but McKay traveled with this strange stuff that no city person could identify if threatened at knifepoint. And, par for the course, he was aiming toward her with an armload of unfamiliar gear. "Clumsy isn't relevant, because you're not going to do anything but get in and sit back and loll. Close your eyes. Inhale the breeze, the spring day, the speed whipping at your hair. I'm going to do all the sailing work. You're not going to get wet, and you're not going to fall in. I know she looks little, but she's sturdy as a rock.''

She heard the reassuring lecture. But she'd often heard reassuring lectures from her athletic family swearing that some athletic thing was ''easy.'' Besides which, when Mc-Kay stepped closer and started putting his hands on her, she was promptly diverted from remembering what she was worried about. Almost. ''If sailing is so safe, how come you're putting a life jacket on me?''

''Lift your arms. There's a girl. And I'm inclined to tell you that anyone who goes sailing with me wears a life jacket, cut-and-dried—and that *is* cut-and-dried, but it's not the whole truth. The *real* reason I'm putting a life vest on you is that it gives me such a great excuse to get my hands on your breasts. And honestly, Lexie. You're smart enough to have figured that out before now.''

''Well, I did, but I was trying to save your pride by not mentioning it. I mean, you have to be the only man alive hot to get his hands on a couple of 34 AA's. Didn't anyone let you know that this is a Big Boob culture?''

''To each his own. I'll take quality over quantity. However…I meant to bring this up before…but if you don't want me coming onto you all the time, it'd help a bunch if you'd behave yourself.''

''*Me?* Behave *myself?*''

''Yeah, you. The one with her hands on my butt.''

She glanced over his shoulder, and there they were. Her hands. Fingers splayed tightly on his butt. ''I was trying to steady myself,'' she said loftily. ''You pulled me off balance when you were fitting on the life jacket.''

''Yeah, right.'' Just for a moment—a razor-fast moment—his gaze turned sober. ''I keep telling myself that we have to quit this.''

"I tell myself that, too."

"We're both grown-ups and we're both too damn old to think teasing this way is going to stay fun for long."

"Yup," she concurred, trying out his Western drawl.

"There's no way you'd like this country life for long. And no matter what I might want to do, I have Sammy, and that's that. So I don't know what either of us thinks we're doing."

She heard him. She'd always heard him. He never even entertained the idea of her liking the country life and fitting in—because of course she wouldn't. But that kind of rational thinking hadn't stopped her from savoring every single miniscule second she had with him—and it didn't now. "Beats me. I don't know what we're doing, either." She squeezed his rump. "God, you are so cute."

He sighed. Heavily and evocatively. Then removed his hands from her boobs and finished zipping up the life vest. "Okay. So we're going to continue being immature about this."

"It looks like it."

"I like my hands on you." He took a small, delicate bite of her neck, as if to illustrate that he liked his mouth on her, too.

"I like your hands on me, too." Since they were courting trouble faster than two-year-olds left near an unsupervised cookie jar, she figured she might as well push it a little more. "You think we should sleep together?"

"I think it'd be damn dumb." He started striding toward the water and the boat, not seeming aware that his hand was hooked with hers and he was dragging her with him. "Damn it, Lex. If you were just some woman, I'd already have slept with you."

"What's that supposed to mean?"

"A fair number of women come here for straight recreation. Any kind. All kinds. And it's not often I play that game, but I don't feel guilty when I do. It's mutual."

"There's a point to your telling me this?" she asked
dryly.

"Yeah. You're not like anyone else. I keep telling myself
that it's daft to feel anything but casual toward you but you
don't give off casual vibrations, either. I have this bad feeling that we're going to end up together some night. But I'm
going to be pissed—downright furious mad—if you get hurt
out of this. And I'm not kidding."

"Well, I don't like the idea of hurting you, either." And
Lexie thought he could be. Cash wasn't as tough and macho
as he let on. She'd seen him with the squirt too many times
not to know exactly what a loving heart he had. And what
a lonely one. "Maybe if we just keep being so annoyingly
honest about this, it'll work out," she suggested.

Truthfully she thought their being honest was one of the
problems. Cash had integrity up the wazoo and then some.
It was one of the things that hopelessly drew her to him.
How could she *not* care about someone who was such a
strong true-blue good guy?

Temporarily, though, Cash hurled a way more critical
problem in her path than sex and love.

How to survive a sailing lesson.

Standing in the spanking-chill breeze, she endured the vo-
cabulary test first. Cash never let anybody get into a new
activity without a salad course of education before the main
meal. So on he ranted, about the hull. Rigger. Tiller. Cen-
terboard. Mainsail. Bailing can.

"The bailing can I could have figured out all on my
own," Lexie said wryly. "But I didn't quite understand—
which of these poles is the boom?"

It was a bad mistake to ask a question, because he immediately, patiently, went through the whole lesson again.
After which he seemed to think she wanted to know how to
put up the rainbow sail and all the fancy words involved in
that job. "The first thing we have to do is bend on the

sail...then put in battens...clear the mainsheet...then we look aloft and hoist sail...."

"Are you going to be annoyed if I can't remember all this stuff?"

"Annoyed with you, madam? As if that could happen in this lifetime," Cash said gallantly, and then, "Touch those knots and you die. Just hold your horses. Sheesh. You're as impatient as a little kid. I thought you were worried about tipping over."

"I am, I am. But by the time you get finished with all the education and safety lessons, I'll be an old woman of 120 who's too decrepit to hobble onto the ship."

"Boat. Not ship. And I have a bad feeling that when you're 120, you'll probably still be giving me grief. Maybe even more grief, hard as that is to imagine."

But it caught her imagination, what it would be like to be with him when she was an old woman and he was an old man. Still, teasing her the whole time, he got her settled in the boat, gave her something to hold, told her not to touch anything else or risk real trouble, and then they were out on the water. He did something to make the sail catch the wind and wow, that was it—suddenly they were skimming along, racing the breeze, the water dancing with diamonds and his eyes dancing with laughter and just plain-old joy of life.

The wind whipped her hair in her face and stung some color in her cheeks. And Cash kept playing with the sail, bringing her in, then out, turning the boat around on a dime, then aiming her down-lake at race-for-hell speeds that exhilarated both of them. Her heart suddenly clutched when she realized that he was happy. Really happy. Happy with the boat, the day, the moment, but also happy with her. And it was suddenly easy to picture them doing this forty years from now, him with stark white hair and spiderweb wrinkles around his eyes, her with a chunky stomach and parchment skin. Him, giving her orders. Her, giving him sass. Him, needing his fresh air every day not to go crazy. Her, needing her daily dose of couch-time and cozy lamplight to be content, but slowly coaxed into inhaling some outside fresh air, too, because tarnation, he was so damn much fun to be with that even exercise didn't seem like that terrible a punishment.

He wasn't touching her.

She wasn't touching him.

But in that second, Lexie knew that she wasn't risking falling in love with him. It was too late. She already had. And this horrible, huge, feeling she had for him...she was petrified that she just may never feel it again. It was for him and him alone, and she kept thinking *Don't ruin this. Just let it be. Don't let him know how much you care and risk him getting freaked out and losing him. Just inhale how good this feels and savor it.*

"Lexie..." In spite of the exuberant wind and the whistle of the sails, Cash was suddenly looking at her. Suddenly whispering something to her in a really low voice. And she thought, ohmygod, maybe he felt it, too? Maybe for once in her life, she'd finally found someone else. Maybe she wasn't the only one suffering that winsome, wild, wonderful feeling. That...love. That something so special that she wanted to burst with it.

But his voice had turned so soft, that she couldn't quite hear him, not over the wind. "Say it again?" she asked, just as softly.

"I said, look behind you. But turn your head really, really slowly."

Naturally she whipped her head around faster than the speed of light. Her jaw dropped even faster. At that specific instant they were into a curve and couldn't possibly be thirty feet from the south shore. She saw something big and brown at the lake edge, but it took a second for her to figure out what it was. A moose. And the comically ungainly critter had apparently decided to wade in and take a bath, oblivious to the humans and their pitifully small sailing rig.

"Cash, *look*—!" The moose was so close. She'd never imagined being this close to a wild animal, much less one this big, and his clumsy splashing and gawkly gait both fascinated her and made her laugh. But then the sail fluttered into her line of vision.

"Lexie, sit still—"

"He's so incredible—do you see the way he—"

"Lexie! You can't stand up in a boat this sm—"

She wasn't exactly *standing*. She'd just whirled around and crouched on her knees so that she could see beyond the sail edge. Only her foot slipped. And she grabbed at something to hold on. And the next thing she knew, the pewter-cold water was reaching out to swallow her up, completely drowning out the sound of Cash both laughing and yelling at her.

"And then what happened, Cash? After she fell in and you fell in and the boat tipped over?"

"Hey, didn't I tell you this story four times already?"

"Yeah, but I like it better every time." Sammy grinned, even as Cash was tucking in the covers and trying to con him into sleeping—again.

"Well, we were in the south end of the lake, and you know how shallow it is. Lexie could have stood up at anytime, but instead, she starts shrieking the instant she hits the water, saying she's gonna drown and it's so cold."

"Oh yeah, yeah, I can picture her yelling just like that." Sammy crossed his hands behind his head, clearly delighted to hear the repeated refrain of the story.

"And you know the Hobie. It's almost impossible to flip her over, but once she has, she's a bitc—um, she's extremely difficult to turn right side up." Cash knew how easily Sammy picked up off-color words, but sometimes he forgot to watch his language. "Anyway...I had my hands full, trying to get the boat upright at the same time Lexie was yelling to beat the band, and—"

They both heard the telephone jangle from the other room. "It's okay. Go get it, go get it. But come back and tell me the rest again," Sammy wheedled.

"All right..." He should have just turned out the lights and insisted on saying good-night, but the squirt really didn't look all that ready to close down for the night yet. And Sammy was too darn prone to insomnia and sleep disorders not to try to make his bedtime as stress free as possible. "I'll be back as soon as I can. Promise."

Cash hustled to the nearest phone, in his bedroom. The instant he picked up the receiver, though, he wished he'd ignored the call altogether. There was a woman's voice on the other end. A familiar woman's voice.

"Hannah...you haven't called it months." He didn't try sitting on the king-size bed. Once he heard his sister's voice, he automatically started pacing. His bedroom window overlooked the west woods, where rabbits were starting to sneak out and munch on greenery in the bluesy twilight shadows. He thought that Lexie would undoubtedly shriek with delight if she saw the rabbits, no different than she had for the moose.

Once the thought of Lexie crossed his mind, a picture of her kiss-softened mouth nudged into his memory banks, too. He wanted to think about *her,* not his sis. Something was happening between him and Lex—something that was powerful and compelling and increasingly driving him nuts.

The immediate problem of his sister, though, simply wouldn't wait. "So how are you?" he asked civilly.

"I'm fine. I'd have called before, but I was ill."

"Uh-huh." He'd have given her sympathy, except that he'd already heard that excuse. A dozen times. "Where are you?"

"Right now, Houston."

"Oh, yeah?" Last time it had been Durango. Before that, Laramie. "You're getting further and further south."

"Warmer. And cheaper to heat. But more to the point, it's where the work is," she said defensively. "How is he?"

Cash didn't waste time asking who she meant. "He's about to go to sleep, but I know for positive he's still awake right now. Don't tell me you're willing to talk to him?"

"If you're going to start with me—"

"I'm not, I'm not." He pinched the skin between his brows. Getting sarcastic or mad at Hannah never worked, which he should have known. More to the point, it didn't help. "I just wanted you to know that Sammy was right in the next room and convenient, if you wanted to talk to him."

"Maybe, in a minute. But he is the reason I called, Cash, so I could hear from you how he is. Does he miss me? I'll bet he doesn't even remember me."

"He remembers you," Cash said shortly. "Are you doing all right? Job wise, life wise?"

"Yeah, well, there's always a job. And this one in Houston looks like it just might last a while. Good opportunity. I might go back to school."

"That'd be great." He didn't say more, because he'd heard the back-to-school goal before, too.

"You don't believe me, but I even got the course curriculum this time."

"Uh-huh."

"And I'm not fooling around with any men, if that's what you're thinking. I'm really working to get my life back together—"

"I wasn't going to criticize, Hannah. I was just trying to ask how you were. But if you're going to talk to Sammy—"

"Maybe that isn't a good idea," she said swiftly.

"So…you're calling because you need money."

"Well…things are going well. But I do want to go back

to school. And this is a new job, new city, so I do happen to be a little cash-strapped. I wasn't going to ask you, though—''

''Uh-huh. Well, I'll tell you…I'm taking the phone into Sammy's room, so you can talk to him…and then I'll talk with you afterward.'' It was bribery, pure and simple, but Cash knew his sister got the message. She had to talk to Sammy and she had to be nice—if she wanted any moola out of him.

When he strode into Sammy's room with the phone, the urchin was still wide-awake and charged up, waiting for him, his eyes brimming with hopeful enthusiasm in the soft lamplight. ''First, a phone call.'' Cash covered the receiver, yet still he whispered. ''It's your mom. You don't have to talk to her if you don't want to, sport, but if you do…''

Sammy bounded out of the bed faster than a rocket. Oh, yeah, he wanted to talk to his mom. He lived and breathed for the few times in a year Hannah could be bribed into calling—or Hannah needed enough money to have a reason to call and try bilking her brother.

Cash thought to give the kid some privacy, but he knew his sister too well, so he hovered in the doorway, not eavesdropping, but watching the kid's face in case anything upsetting got said. The call seemed to go smoothly enough, until Sammy suddenly blurted out, ''Are you coming to see me soon, Mom?''

Cash couldn't hear what Hannah said, but Sammy's face fell a thousand feet and then some. ''Sure, sure, I unnerstand,'' Sammy said bravely. ''Hey, it's no biggie. Cash and me, we're real busy here, doing guy things and all.''

After the call was over—and Hannah got her promise of a good chunk getting wired her way—Sammy wanted to talk about the sailing lesson with Lexie again. He laughed like before, hounded Cash for a repeat of the details, just like before, and obviously couldn't wait to see Lexie in the morning to start teasing her.

But as Cash could have expected—should have expected—Hannah's call the same as guaranteed that neither of them would get a good night's sleep. He heard the squirt crying in his pillow still at eleven, even though he pretended to be asleep when Cash came in to try to comfort him. And he heard Sammy rustling around his room somewhere around two in the morning, and knew darn well the kid had wet the bed.

Eight

The routine was so familiar that Cash could almost do it in his sleep. He stashed Sammy under a warm shower, and then hustled back to the squirt's room to yank off the sheets and get them started in the washing machine. Two minutes later, he'd hurled on fresh sheets, tucked in the blankets and was back in the bathroom doorway.

Thick, warm steam seeped around the shower curtain. Sleepy steam. Through groggy eyes Cash squinted at the hall clock, yawned and leaned his head against the doorjamb until he heard the sound of the faucets being turned off. Then he stepped in, and handed a big, thirsty towel to the small fingers groping in the steamy air for the towel rack.

The head promptly popped out. "You didn't have to wait around, Cash. I don't need anybody to put me back to bed."

"I know you could do that yourself, slugger. You're my man. I just wanted to wait around for you, that's all." Cash saw the glistening hair, the glistening skin…the glistening eyes.

Sammy grabbed the towel and started rubbing his skinny body. Cash dropped another towel over his head. "This is not a big deal," he said firmly.

"I didn't say it was." The kid's tone was defensive. Ornery. Cash knew better than to buy it.

"But it bugs you."

First silence. But then Sammy got around to offering a grudging, "Yeah. Maybe." The towel came off the head, but the head stayed down. "I thought it was over. Like that it would never happen to me again and I could quit worrying about it. It'd been a long time."

"I know it had." Just like Cash knew that's when the bed wetting thing had started for the urchin. Another night, just like this one, when everything had been going fine—until his sister called. And emotionally tore the kid up, the same damn way.

"Lexie said she wet the bed when she was a little girl. Only she wasn't so little. She was too old to be doing it. Like me."

Cash rubbed him down more thoroughly with the towel, because Sammy invariably yanked on pj's when his skin was still clammy. He was careful not to hug him, though. The kid's shoulders were as thin and stiff as a soldier's. Cash had no idea what a real dad would do under the circumstances, but he knew about pride, knew the kid struggled to find his. Whether he wanted to gather up the boy and hug the hell out of him didn't matter. Cash just sensed that it would hurt more than help.

"If Lexie told you that . .then you know someone else had this problem, huh? You're not the only one."

"Yeah." A gusty, lonely sigh. "It *did* make me feel better, that she told me. She's okay."

"And I'll bet she told you the problem wasn't about age. Just like I keep trying to tell you."

"Yeah, yeah. I know."

Maybe Sammy had heard it before, but Cash still tried again. "A lot of things can cause you to lose control when you're sleeping—but it's nothing at all like being a baby. In fact, it's specifically the kind of problem that *only* an older kid can get. You couldn't even have this problem if you were way younger." Or that was one of the strategies the pediatrician had suggested trying on Sammy.

"Yeah, well." Sammy had had enough toweling off. He hurled both at the rack, then loped past him toward the bedroom, forgetting the pj's on the counter altogether, his head still drooping dejectedly but not quite so alley-low. "At least it's just us."

"Come again?" Cash couldn't quite hear the muffled whisper.

"At least nobody knows about it but you and me. Just us guys. We don't need wimmen, do we, Cash? Not as long as we got each other. If you don't have wimmen around, you don't have to worry about being embarrassed so much. Right?"

Eventually the urchin got snuggled down again, but by the time Cash threw himself back in his own bed, he was as wide-awake as a porcupine with an itch. He could scratch the itch—but not without risking a sharp poke in a vulnerable spot. And the itch, of course, was for Lexie.

He closed his eyes, trying to sleep, but it was impossible to rest when his pulse was still pumping adrenaline. Sammy really was having less and less of a problem with a wet bed. Still, maybe it was an omen that Hannah had called Sammy this particular night, an omen that his bed-wetting problem had reoccurred because it reminded Cash of how fragile the kid could be.

It didn't matter how much he felt increasingly drawn to Lexie. Sammy was his responsibility. The kid would unquestionably be hurt if Cash hooked up with a woman who didn't stay. Maybe he should quit this with Lexie. Quit falling for her. Quit caring. Quit taking delight in her spirit and her clumsiness and her big, gorgeous orphan eyes…and her flat chest…and her mouth…and what she'd looked like when she'd capsized the boat, shrieking at him and laughing and caterwauling about how they were both going to drown….

Cash started grinning in the darkness. And just as abruptly, forced a big wedge of a scowl on his brow. This was *exactly* his problem with her. Every time they were together, he felt this building lunge of emotion pull at him. Enough to make him believe that he wouldn't be bored by her if they lived together for two hundred years. Enough to believe they had enough chemistry to survive—and thrive— even longer than that. Enough to recognize that he felt something for Lexie that no other woman had ever stirred in him.

Only Sammy's innocent words about "embarrassment" now came back to haunt him. The kid really got an unpleasant knot on the truth sometimes. But it *was* true. A man didn't risk getting embarrassed if he just avoided the depth of intimacy altogether. Sammy wouldn't risk getting loved. And neither could he. If both kept running a hundred miles an hour away from any female who threatened 'em with that dangerous four letter *L* word.

Of course it wasn't *any* female who threatened them. It was Lexie.

In all this time, there'd only been Lexie who had gotten under either McKay's craw…a thought that was still pushing on Cash's peace of mind when he heard the distant sound of knocking from his living room front door.

He checked the bedside clock—which registered the ungodly hour of 3:30 a.m. The time was worrisome enough to make him vault out of bed and swiftly yank on a pair of jeans. Obviously nobody would be pounding on the door at this hour unless it were an emergency, so mentally he was already skimming through the possibilities of problems.

Own a lodge like this, being on call for 24 and 7 was just the way it was. If a guest got sick, they called him. If a bear wandered in the yard, he was supposed to be the bear version of a ghostbuster. And though Keegan and George rarely bugged him in the off hours, if there was something serious—like an electrical problem or a fire—he expected to be rousted from bed to take care of it.

By the time he sprinted barefoot toward the front door, his mind had quit flipping through possibilities and was just trying to get an edge sharpened and awake. He was prepared for just about anything except pulling open the door and finding Lexie.

Because women had always been the bane of his life, right off he could see that she'd dressed to tip him over the complete edge.

She was wearing paisley silk pajamas—damn woman even had designer pj's—but there were no socks or slippers; her face was naked of makeup and her hair bobbing in a sleepy, curling fuzz around her face. In one second flat he knew she'd just climbed out of bed. In two seconds flat, he'd altered the vision into a fantasy of what both of them might have, could have, wanted to, just might do in same-said-bed. His heart promptly started slamming. It slammed even harder when his gaze accidentally focused on her small, bare mouth.

"Cash? Could I talk to Sammy?"

"Sammy?" *Sammy?* She wanted the kid and not him? A balloon couldn't deflate this fast from a direct puncture wound. Not that she'd hurt his feelings—badly—but he squinted down at her. "Lexie, you're not having one of your anxiety attacks, are you? You do realize what time it is?"

She nodded her head vigorously. "Almost 4:00 a.m. I know. And normally, I'd never wake a child for anything at this hour. But he's out of school now, so he could sleep in later, yes? The thing is, Martha sneaked into my room and climbed on my bed just a few minutes ago. And the next thing I knew, she was starting to have her puppies. And I just thought that Sammy would really like to see—''

He pivoted around at jet speed. ''I'll get him.''

An hour later, Cash was feeling more sorry for himself than an abandoned cat in a rainstorm. Everybody was having a good time but him.

This puppy-birthing debacle was going to cost him a new mattress—which wasn't exactly an item you could parcel-post to this neck of Idaho. Furthermore, since neither of the birthing support staff were willing to leave Martha even for a second, obviously Cash had to volunteer for all the fetch-and-carry jobs—like bringing a water bowl for the mama dog, and two glasses of milk for the human support staff, then sleeping bags, then spare pillows, on and on.

Truth to tell, none of that stuff really bothered him. It was the sleeping arrangements that put his nose out of joint.

He'd dreamed of sleeping with Lexie. He admitted it. Dreamed in surround sound and digital technological detail. Dreamed often. Dreamed erotically and exotically. But he'd never once dreamed—in the farthest stretches of his imagination—that when he finally got to spend the night with her, it would be the pint-sized squirt who got to snuggle with her, and him who got the straight chair in the far corner.

''You think she'll have more?'' Sammy whispered to Lexie.

The two of them were huddled in a double sleeping bag on the floor, along with extra blankets and pillows. They had the prize view of the bed, where Martha had the Queen-of-Sheba lounging site. Unfortunately that ended it for the sleeping bag and lounging sites, which meant that Cash was stuck in the chair. Rain gushed down the windows, streaming silver ribbons, making her bedroom feel colder than well water and only the occasional streak of lightning illuminating the dead-of-night darkness. The last lightning streak had revealed Martha's limpid wet eyes, and the two heads huddled together just below her.

"I don't know, Sammy," Lexie whispered back. "It's been a while now. Maybe that's it. Four seems like a pretty good-sized litter to me."

"I don't care if she has more. I'm happy with four. I'm so happy I could just jump off the roof," Sammy assured her sleepily. "It's just that I don't want to go to sleep in case she has another one. I don't want to miss anything."

"Me, either," Lexie agreed. Cash watched her brush back his son's hair and tuck the sleeping bag a little closer around his neck. Something clutched low in his belly. Not lust, for a change. It was just some strange, stupid, poignant thing, seeing her make such a momlike gesture. Such a loving gesture. Particularly when the two had been whispering together like conspiring criminals.

Truth to tell, he could have forced 'em to move over on the floor, but hell. He didn't want to break the spell. It would be like taking Mutt away from Jeff, or ripping peanut butter away from jelly. Lexie and Sam had both inhaled being part of the puppies being born as if it were the most important thing that had ever happened in either of their lives. And damn, but maybe Hannah hadn't soured Sammy forever on reaching out to another female, because it sure as hell looked like he was crazy for Lexie. Not crazy like in little-boy-crush, but crazy wonderful as in loving her for real, trusting her.

It would all be just fine—if his corner of the room weren't colder than a well digger's ankle. And if they weren't having such a great time without him.

"Did you notice, Sammy? It didn't seem to hurt her to have the babies. She seemed to know just what to do."

"Yeah. I was afraid she'd whine or cry or like that. Or

she'd die or something. Or maybe that she'd see a puppy come out and go away because she didn't want it.''

Cash caught his breath, but he heard her answering the kid, so gently and carefully that it was obvious Lexie was sensitive to his complicated feelings about his mom. ''Well, I didn't see the first puppy, but we've both seen how she treated all the others, haven't we? She was cleaning them off and loving them right from the first minute she saw them. Maybe something could make her leave her babies, hon. But it's hard to imagine her wanting to do that.''

''Well, they haven't caused her any trouble yet. But we'll be here then, won't we, Lexie? So if they're a lot of trouble, we can help take care of them and they won't be alone.''

''Yeah, we could. And if Martha needs something, we could help her, too. You know what, Sammy? I almost didn't wake you. I really didn't know what this was going to be like, and I didn't want you to see Martha if she was going to be in a lot of pain or really miserable.''

Sammy's profile was silhouetted against another strike of lightning, his face peeled up to hers. ''Lexie, I'd have killed you if you hadn't come got me. This was the neatest thing I ever saw in my whole life. And she's my dog. So she probably wanted me here and all. To pet her and stuff.''

''I thought she wanted you here to pet her, too,'' Lexie agreed gravely. And then yawned. ''Got any more M&M's in your pj pocket?''

''Hey,'' Cash interjected.

''Good grief. What am I thinking. Candy at four in the morning—how disgusting!'' Lexie said in an appalled tone and then ducked her head against slugger's head. They both giggled. Then chewed. Then turned around to flash a matched set of guileless smiles at him.

''If there's the slightest chance you two are through goofing off, I really think it might be a good idea to try to catch a little sleep before dawn.''

"Well, shoot," Lexie grumbled to Sammy. "Your dad's right. It is just a hair on the late side—"

"I'm not leaving Martha," Sammy wailed.

"Hey, I didn't say anything about your leaving Martha. But you could lay down here in the sleeping bag. And I'll bet the bank that your dad'll lay down with you, because something just tells me he's found this a pretty special experience himself. And I never meant to monopolize this whole deal, when Martha is your dog and your dad's. Not mine. So, I'll…" She hesitated, then forged on swiftly, "I'll just take some blankets down to the living room and bunk down on one of the couches."

"But, Lexie, then you won't get to see it if Martha decides to have another puppy," Sammy objected.

"That's okay. I've seen the other ones. And your dad'll be here, so he'll watch over Martha so you can sleep."

Cash finally got a word in. "Nope."

"No?" Lexie's face peeled toward his.

Sheesh. Did the two of them really think he was that dumb? As if he could fail to notice how braced Lexie was to get kicked out of the family group? "No," he repeated gruffly. "I think that plan is lousy. You two are already all curled up in that big sleeping bag. I don't see any reason for anyone to move."

"Well, of course there is," Lexie said sensibly. "You have to be freezing over there in that corner. And I've had Sammy all this time to enjoy the birthing thing with him. It's your turn. And I'm not part of—"

"Yeah, you are part of this. Part of us."

"Yeah." Sammy echoed Cash's big blustery voice. "Come on down here with us, Cash. Don't let Lexie go anywhere. We'll all just sleep here until morning."

"You guys both know I have insomnia. There's really no chance I could go to sleep, anyway—"

Uh-huh. Once Cash plunked down on the floor with

them—about two seconds after he sat down, in fact—both of them were out for the count faster than an arrow could hit a bull's-eye, Sammy cuddled against Lexie's shoulder, her chin bowed against the boy's head.

Cash sighed, and then quieter than a prayer, he ruffled one extra blanket over both of them and made sure there were no loose air pockets. Then he pushed a pillow under his own cheek. The three of them were lying like peas in a pod, Lexie's arm around Sammy's waist, his arm around Lexie's waist. The two of them were already emitting little breathy snores.

Not him. Naturally, he had to force himself to keep his own eyes pried open.

Somebody around here had to keep vigil.

Martha, on the bed, met his gaze from her superior mattress height. She hadn't been paying him much attention. She'd seemed to want the other humans around, making little whiny sounds and tail-thumping when Sammy petted her or Lexie praised her…and God knew the dog had chosen to whelp on Lexie's bed, so there wasn't much question Martha considered Lexie on her special human list. Him, though, who knew?

But in the dark pre-dawn fog, Martha's limpid brown eyes met his, as if in acknowledgement that neither dared sleep when they had so many charges to watch out for. The pups, Cash had to admit, were a wonder. The birth hadn't been a pretty process and the puppies no cuter than scalped rats, but Martha had cleaned 'em up, nuzzled 'em together in a heap by their food source, and bent down to look at them every few minutes as if they were as precious and priceless as diamonds.

Hell, Cash thought they were, too—not as precious as *his* two charges, mind you. But there was this huge, overwhelming feeling swelling inside of him. Bursting inside of him.

Splitting his heart wide-open, and somehow allowing that old nemesis of his in. Love. Love for Lexie. For how she was with Sammy, with him, how she was in their lives, what she brought to him and Sammy both.

All the reasons he worried about becoming involved with her were real. But for the first time he considered that—possibly—he'd been hiding behind Sammy. No, he didn't want to risk hurting the kid. But every time Cash saw the two together, Sammy was shining under her care and attention.

All these years, it had been so easy to live the life of a coward—to avoid getting hurt by using Sammy as the excuse to avoid entanglements with women. And yeah, slugger would get hurt if Lexie took off on them. Just maybe, though, the kid would be even more hurt if he never had a chance to be close to her.

The rain finally stopped. The satin black night finally lightened. The early-morning chill was enough to nip his toes. The blanket wasn't long enough to cover his feet, not when he had to keep the other two warmly covered in those early-morning seriously freezing hours. But then came the dawn light. Silver soft, then pearl with a golden kiss to it. As soon as there was light, any light, he found himself staring at Lexie's sleeping face like a man mesmerized.

It didn't matter what a short time he'd known her.

It didn't matter what risks he had to take.

Cash had the terrible feeling that he was falling for her. Hard. And that Sammy was already attached—even harder. Which meant that he was coming up against a rock and a hard place.

Cash couldn't imagine Lexie wanting to stay, but this had already gone too far. He was in no hustle to use that worrisome love word, but a man had no way to win a woman without wooing her. Either he took the risk or for damn sure he would lose her.

* * *

Lexie's eyes snapped open, her heart pounding as if a sudden sense of danger had abruptly wakened her.

Naturally there was no danger. The night's drenching rain had turned into drenching bright sunlight—not dawn light, but full get-up-and-go daylight. The birdsong was practically as loud as a rock band, with maniacally happy robins and blue jays fluttering around the windows. One noisy blue jay landed on the sill and stared in the window like a nosy voyeur…and suddenly Lexie froze.

It seemed the blue jay knew something she didn't, because she abruptly realized that she was sleeping with two males. One large. One small. And since everyone seemed to be completely clothed, the situation wasn't exactly startling. Except to her. She could see the bird and sunlight just fine through her left eye. As it happened, her right eye and cheek were plastered against Cash's neck. And her bent knee was tucked between his legs—certainly there was a layer of sleeping bag and blankets and clothes between them but the electric awareness kicking through her pulse was distinctly sexual. She'd have recognized McKay if she were blindfolded and hog-tied. Her hormones knew him *that* well. And the thing was, Sammy was right there, his bitsy little butt trying to snuggle against her back.

Swiftly she pivoted her head. Sammy shifted, but he certainly didn't waken. The squirt was snoring as loud as any grown-up. Just above them, Martha's snout was hanging over the bed edge, her patient dog-eyes watching over them all. Her new babies were all snoozing in a heap. Outside, Lexie heard the muted, distant sound of laughter—the whole world was up and around. Except for them.

She took a quick breath and then tried easing out of the sleeping bag an inch. Cash promptly tucked an arm around her even tighter. She waited, her pulse drumming, and then tried to sneak out another couple of inches. His arm snuggled her closer yet.

"G'morning, love," he murmured.

Again, she froze, confounded by that "love"—and even more by that intimately low, sexy baritone. His eyes suddenly opened, bluer than the ocean, roaming her face with a lover's familiarity. The way a lover would talk. The way a lover would look at her. It was enough to give a girl an anxiety attack.

"Good morning," she whispered back cautiously, and then tried easing out another inch.

His hand tightened. His smile loosened. "Quite a night, wasn't it?"

She stared at him blankly. Quite often, she woke up crabby, at least until she'd had a double dose of caffeine. But not Cash. He always woke up sunny and perky and aware so by now he had to realize that Sammy was right there with them.

Actually he glanced beyond her and saw Sammy. For sure. Yet his smile only broadened. "I could give birth with you anytime."

Martha's tail thumped, as if she thought he was talking about her. Lexie wasn't so sure what he was talking about. "Thank you. I think."

"Best experience Sammy's had in a blue moon."

She relaxed. A little. She'd relax a whole lot more if he'd loosen his arm. She wasn't much on snuggling with two males in the same room, particularly when one was drastically underage. Cash wasn't, of course, snuggling exactly. He wasn't touching anything inappropriate. And everybody was covered up to the neck. The sleepover had a perfectly natural cause because of Martha's puppies.

But Lexie still felt her heart engaged in a dozen intimate levels. Even if her hormones were clanging a five-alarm fire strictly for Cash, an overabundance of maternal instincts seemed to well inside her for Sammy at the same time. She had, after all, slept with her two favorite males in the universe. Geezle beezle. When had they come to matter so desperately much to her? "I'm getting up," she muttered firmly.

But then she didn't move. Cash didn't argue, didn't stop her from moving that time. He did nothing but rest cheek-to-cheek on the same pillow, looking at her, seeming to savor her sleep-tousled hair and flushed skin and bare mouth. No one looked at her that way. Before. Ever. As if she were more precious than diamonds. As if she were being...claimed. Body. Soul. Everywhere he looked, she felt his possession in black ink.

He was rattling her. Badly. What the Sam Hill was going on here?

"Cash," she hissed, "I have to get up, get dressed."

"Okay." But he didn't move.

"The whole lodge is probably up. You're never late for anything. The whole place will be worried about you, wondering where you are."

"Probably." He agreed, but he still didn't move. He wasn't exactly stopping her from climbing out of the sleeping bag. But he wasn't moving himself. And he was still looking at her in that same intense, compelling, strange way.

"What's wrong with you, McKay?"

"Nothing, honey."

First love, now honey? "You don't feel well?" she asked with genuine concern.

He responded with a broad smile. "I can't remember feeling better...although I have to admit, when I wake up next to you next time, I hope it's under a little less crowded circumstances."

That was it. She could not only feel a private flush skidding from her throat to her cheeks, but Cash could undoubtedly see it. Faster than a heartbeat, she skinnied out from under the sleeping bag and blankets, and galloped for the bathroom. She had no idea what was wrong with the man, but surely over the long day ahead, if she just gave him some time and space, he'd come to his senses and start behaving normally again.

Nine

By dinnertime, Lexie was fit to be tied. She'd been positive that Cash's loverlike behavior would disappear the minute they got in public. Instead his attitude had only gotten worse through the day. Initially she felt certain that he must be catching a flu—either that, or suffering from dementia—so she'd shut up out of kindness. It seemed cruel to kick a man when he was down, after all. Obviously no one in life chose to have a screw loose. And although she'd never suspected Cash of being two pennies short of a nickel in his brain bank, who knew?

Duh.

She'd tried ignoring his lapses in sane behavior all day, and it had gotten her nowhere. She wasn't running out of patience, exactly. But she was extremely close to either getting an anxiety attack or slapping him. Temporarily she felt uncertain which would be the more helpful solution.

"Hey, Lexie, are you listening?"

"Of course, I was listening, punkin." She smiled at Sammy across the dinner table, although truthfully she hadn't heard a word he'd said. They'd been talking about the boat incident, how she'd gotten so excited over seeing the moose that she'd managed to tip over the little sailboat. That part of the conversation she remembered clearly. Only it was at that point that Cash, walking toward the kitchen, had passed the back of her chair and paused to squeeze her shoulders.

It was the same kind of demented thing he'd done all day. Technically there was nothing weird about his touching her shoulders. There was no crime involved. No overt intimacy, either. But it was the *way* he did it—the way lovers had to be in touch every couple of seconds or they started going bonkers. He was just ambling toward the kitchen. There was no reason in the universe for him to pause and suddenly cuddle her shoulders in that private little squeeze and look at her as if the sun had dropped out of the sky and into her eyes.

"Because moose are dangerous. I'm not kidding, Lexie. They look so clumsy and goofy that it's hard to be afraid of 'em, you know? But you don't want to get close. Just ask Cash, if you don't believe me. Especially in spring like now. Because if a mama moose thinks you're anywhere near her babies, she'll charge you. I'm not just making this up."

"I believe you completely," Lexie assured him. "I promise not to go up to any more mooses. Or is it moosi? What's the plural of moose, anyway?"

"Maybe it's like mouse, mice…moose, meece." Jed Harper, the pilot, had popped in just in time for dinner. He was flying two of Cash's guests out tonight, Bob and Winn Roush, the insurance guys from Cleveland who'd been here all last week. The Roushes and Sammy both laughed at this spelling suggestion.

"You're so silly, Mr. Harper," Sammy said. "There's no such word as meece! Didn't you know that?"

"Nope. I guess it's a good thing you're going to school, huh? So you can teach the old fogies like me some real spelling? Lexie..."

Lexie politely turned her head when Jed spoke her name, but whatever he said never registered. She suffered another blankness-of-the-brain problem—and for the same reason. Cash and Keegan were both strolling in from the kitchen, carting dessert, Cash carrying the plates and Keegan's hands occupied with both a fresh pie and a cherry-apple cake. After dropping the goodies, both men walked back to their seats.

Except that Cash made a slight detour. As he passed her chair, he bent down. She felt his lips skim a whiskery, shivery caress on her nape as he passed by. A kiss. A wicked, elicit, lover-type kiss. In front of everyone at the dinner table, for Pete's sake. In front of Sammy, besides. And even before Cash had calmly reseated himself, her brain had flown to Poughkeepsie and her tongue felt glued to the roof of her mouth.

"Lexie, did you hear me?" Jed asked again.

"I'm sorry, I must have missed what you said—"

"I was just remarking how different you look. It's only been a few weeks since I first flew you here, but something is really different. I keep trying to pin down what it is..."

Maybe he couldn't pin it down, but Lexie knew exactly what he was talking about. Across the room hung an old antique mirror in a leather frame, near the door—a place where someone could check to make sure they weren't leaving the dining room with lettuce hanging between their teeth. It was also a location where she kept accidentally catching her own appalling reflection. And Jed was right. In less than three weeks, her appearance had drastically changed.

For the dinner hour, she'd typically changed into her version of casual clothes—a nice, V-neck silk sweater in a pale blue, paired with loose, silk navy-blue slacks. Only it seemed that she was still wearing Sammy's borrowed grubby tennies. And because she'd forgotten to bring the belt for these particular slacks, Keegan had loaned her this strange leather one that you could pull up tight to any size. And then Cash had caught her shivering and draped his black-and-white flannel shirt over her shirt.

In a little more than two weeks, something about this place had completely annihilated Alexandra Jeannine Woolf and turned her into a stranger. The days were so busy that she just couldn't catch enough time to style her hair, so of necessity she was wearing it wash-and-wear. She'd always been stuck with naturally curly hair, but now the loose springy curls were doing whatever they wanted. To her, it was starting to look hopelessly floofy. Her makeup tubes had barely been opened lately, because there was never time for that, either. Only the hair and clothes and lack of makeup weren't really the problem. It was That Other Thing in the mirror.

The glow.

The nonstop glow on her face.

There was more color in her cheeks than if she'd put on cheap blush, and nothing seemed to make it go away.

She had a bad, bad feeling that she knew precisely what that damn glow was caused from, but the worst thing about all these appearance issues was something unexpected. No one seemed to think she looked silly. No one seemed to even notice that nothing went together. People here—Cash—were so damn weird that they made out like she fit in. No matter what she said. No matter what she wore.

This idiocy simply had to stop.

"It's probably lack of sleep that's making me look different," she told Jed. "Cash is running some place here. Last night I either had to sleep on the floor or with five other bodies."

"I beg your pardon, ma'am?" Jed's whiskered jaw dropped in shock...even though he had to see little Sammy chortling at her humor.

"It's the truth. Sammy thankfully brought me a sleeping bag. Otherwise I'd have had to sleep with two males and three other females. And heaven knows where I'm going to find a place to hang my hat tonight."

"I believe we can come up with something, darling."

Lexie whirled around when Cash spoke. She heard the humor in his tone, understood that he was just adding to the conversation, but his use of "darling" was still no joke. It rolled off his tongue like the first strain in a love song, making Sammy suddenly look at him. And Jed.

That's it, Lexie thought morosely, and pushed back her chair. "If you'll all excuse me, I'm going to go check on our ménage à cinq. Sammy, you're welcome to come with me, if you want."

"You bet, you bet!"

"And could I catch you a little later, Cash? Just for a quick word," she said casually.

"You know you can," Cash assured her...in that same sexy, velvet voice.

She felt his eyes on her back as she took off for the stairs—and the puppies—with Sammy. And she had a terrific time with Martha and the pups and Sam. But eventually Sammy started yawning and ambled back downstairs. It would be another hour before he was in bed and asleep, Lexie figured and by that time she'd paced the room a good dozen times *and* pushed up her sleeves, preparing for a fight.

When she heard the knock on the door, she was *ready* to have it out with Mr. Cashner Aaron McKay...but she wasn't expecting to open the door and see him standing there with an armful of tent stakes and debris and heaven-knows-what-all. Eventually she got around to noticing the boyish smile and the conspiratorial wink.

"Now, I know you're annoyed with me and I know why," he said, "but come on. Give me a chance to fix it, okay? Follow me."

She followed him, primarily because she didn't want to argue in a bedroom—in front of the puppies—or out in the hall where others could hear, either. But she was mystified at his leading her downstairs, out the back door of the lodge and to the distant edge of the wooded yard. He'd barely dropped the heap of supplies in his arms before he handed her a flashlight and started working.

"That's all you have to do—hold the light for me, okay?" he asked her genially.

"Hold the light for *what?*"

"Now, Lex. I know we've had trouble finding a sport for you. But it occurred to me that since we obviously need to find a new place for you to sleep tonight—thanks to Martha and the puppies—we should take advantage of the problem and kill two birds with one stone. Give you a place to throw your pillow. And offer you a new sporting experience at the same time."

"Oh, God. Not another sport."

"This is different," he assured her. "This is just camping out."

"You mean camping…as in sleeping outside?"

"Um, that's how camp-outs usually work, honey-love. But unlike all the other sports, this is finally one that you're really going to be able to get into. Trust me. It's not about…athletics. It's about sleeping in the night air. It's about tasting the magic of midnight and feeling the moonbeams and smelling the dew soaking the wildflowers and grass. It's about being close to nature."

"Cash, honest to Pete, I'd rather be close to a potty and a heat register than close to nature."

"Exactly, darling. See how close we are to the lodge? If you want a bathroom, or the kitchen, all you have to do is run inside. Keegan and the staff all know we're here, and so does Sammy, and they all know you can be a little...squeamish...around outside things. No one's going to bug us, because no one wants you worrying that any little sound could be a wolf or a bear. So there's nothing to worry about. I'm putting up the tent, which should only take a couple more minutes, if you'll keep holding the light. Got a double air mattress, so there's no way you'll be sleeping on anything damp or rocky. And I brought down bags, so you'll be snug as a bug in a rug. So to speak. And down pillows—"

"McKay." She couldn't keep the bewilderment out of her tone, and not just for the "honey-love" and the "darling." "You thought I was aggravated because you hadn't 'found a sport' for me? How many times do I have to tell you? It's not your fault—or your responsibility. No one is going to find a sport for me in this life. I'm clumsy as a toad. That's just the way it is."

"But clumsy doesn't apply to camping out, see? It doesn't matter. You don't have to *do* anything to enjoy. By the way, damned if I know what we're going to do about Martha—I assume move her by tomorrow. But Sammy had a stroke about moving her and the puppies today. And I don't think you'll want to sleep on that mattress again, anyway, so I'm moving you downstairs to one of the first floor apartments tomorrow. But for tonight—"

She couldn't hear how he finished that sentence because he was ham ham hammering the tent stakes in, then billowing out this icky green canvas thing that looked like a giant blanket...only it gradually took shape into a stiffer form. A tent form. With a church-steeple V-shape and a cute little screen door and everything. She shook her head like a dog shook off rainwater, hoping to shed her improving mood and get back to her earlier fury.

"McKay. I was *not* aggravated with you about your Silver

Mountain program, or anything to do with athletics or sports.
It was the honey. The love. The darling.'' Her flashlight
abruptly wobbled. ''All those endearments. I don't understand what you're doing.''

''What I'm doing? Well, right now, I'm putting in the last
tent pole, and then opening the front door for madam.'' He
lifted the screen door tent flap, and then made a medieval
knight's courtly flourish, motioning her inside. ''After you,
shorty.''

''After…me?''

''You didn't think I expected you to sleep alone, did you?
And risk your getting scared of the dark? No way, Jose.
Nothing's going to ruin this night for you. I guarantee it.''
He grinned. And after less-than-gallantly nudging her for-
ward, he hurled in the blown-up air mattress, then the giant
sleeping bag and sealed-up pillows, followed by…

Him.

From the back of the teensy tent, Lexie uneasily tugged
on an earlobe. It was pretty dark back there. So dark she
couldn't see his face, but she could hear him unfurling and
setting up the bedding. She needed to say something—obviously—but temporarily her tongue seemed glued to the
roof of her mouth.

All day, it had been the same. Communicating with Cash
had been like trying to reason with the demented. He said
things that sounded logical—but they weren't. He did things
that seemed logical—but they weren't. And he'd been calling her all those loving names, which seemed an extra worrisome measure that he'd lost the rest of his mental marbles.

So okay. Everybody lost it now and then. No biggie,
Lexie kept telling herself. Only she was just mystified how
to try reasoning with him next.

''Listen, Cash,'' she began in her most soothing, understanding voice.

''I'm listening, I'm listening. But just hold up a second,

okay? I can't move around in here with these big boots on. They have to go.'' A thud followed. Then a second thud. ''Wouldn't you like to take off your shoes, too?''

''No. I—no. McKay—yikes!'' She tumbled backward when he inelegantly grabbed her foot, and yanked off both of Sammy's borrowed tennies at the same time.

''You just have to take me as the expert on this particular subject. When we're talking about stocks, I'll listen to you. But when we're talking moving around in a tent—believe me—there's no way you're going to be comfortable in those shoes.''

Suddenly Lexie couldn't swallow. She didn't move, didn't breathe, just tried to see his face in the semidarkness as he finished cuffing off her shoes, dropped them outside, then zipped up the screen tent flap.

The two of them were abruptly cocooned alone...but that was precisely why Lexie didn't want to risk moving or breathing. Her addled brain had finally figured out what was going on here.

Cash wanted to sleep inside. With her. In the itty-bitty tent. And all this messing around had nothing to do with a camping-out exercise and everything to do with a man who wasn't so sure how the Sam Hill to go about seducing her. He'd been trying to warn her what was coming with all those honey-love-darling endearments. For that matter, any woman with a ten-point IQ would likely have added two and two and come up with four long before this.

Not her. She'd known they had chemistry bubbling between them. She'd known what he'd done, what he'd said. But she also knew how adamantly he avoided involvements with women for Sammy's sake, so she'd never expected him to take a risk. Not for her. For that matter, she still wasn't dead sure she wasn't misreading this.

''Cash,'' she asked softly, carefully, ''I'm one of those people who just can't seem to get to the bottom line unless

I can see all the numbers in a column. Which means, sometimes I need things spelled out for me that other people get right away. Which is an awkward way of trying to ask you, um, did you have in mind our sleeping together? For real?''

The shadows kept moving, rustling. The smells of flannel and wool and warm, clean man started to seep through the tent. She caught the glint of a smile. ''I thought we already discussed that part.''

''In a pig's eye,'' she said delicately. ''We haven't discussed anything. You railroaded me down here with a bunch of talk about camping out. Which seemed reasonable to me, considering the other physical tortures you've put me through since I got here—trying to drown me, throw me off cliffs and so on. But the point is, I didn't necessarily have any reason to think you meant something else. Something besides, um, sleeping outside together.''

A sigh. Low and throaty and dominantly, edgily male. ''I'm not real good with words, Alexandra. But I'll do my best to be more clear. I know damn well women like romancing—and deserve it—but I get all confused about that. It seems to me dead wrong and hellish unfair to get a woman you care about all…roiled up…without giving her a vote first. All day I've been trying to give you a chance to say no, or to punch my lights out, depending on which suited you more. But if you want me to get down to the precise nuances of meaning…I didn't have in mind sleeping at all. For you or me. In any way.''

A sudden silence fell between them. A complete silence, the kind that was pregnant with anticipation and nerves. Her nerves seemed so acute that every sense seemed almost painfully sharpened. She could smell wet earth and damp spring leaves and grass. Outside, leaves whispered in the woods, rustling about secrets, gossiping about magic and the spells of spring. Night temperatures were coming, adding a crisp flavor to the air. The sky was a simmering bowl of navy-blues and midnight-blacks, stirring stars and spooning clouds in swirling patterns across the night. An owl hooted. A branch crackled under the footsteps of some small, scampering critter. A frog croaked—awfully close—and kept up that incessant bleating croak the way frogs do when they're crying out in the lonely night for a mate.

Inside the tent, it was still blacker than pitch, but the longer the silence grew between them, the more her pupils adjusted to the dim light. The sprinkle of star shine worked like a distant lamp, highlighting his profile, that strong nose, those deep-set eyes. It seemed to her that she could smell moonshine. And she could see the glow of light in his eyes, searching hers. Asking hers. Waiting.

Tension heated her blood, snapped at her nerves, until she wanted to smack Cash upside the head. The damn man. Maybe she'd known this moment was coming. Maybe she'd hoped. But she'd wanted to be seduced, not given a choice. She'd wanted to be overwhelmed, not asked for permission. This wasn't supposed to be how it went. She wanted to have excuses later—just in case she needed them—and instead McKay was waiting for her answer with stubborn, tenacious patience.

Ask her, a man could have way, *way* too much honor for a woman's good.

And since he was being so damn annoying, she did the only thing she could. Launched herself into his arms.

He landed on his back with an *oommph* and a growl of a sigh. Or maybe that was her growl. Taking charge was a thousand times more empowering than Lexie had ever dreamed of. Yet in her head, it was amazing how her choices reduced to absolute simplicity.

She didn't understand her pull for him. Never had. Maybe never would. She certainly didn't believe that she belonged with him—but then Lexie never expected that. She'd stopped believing years before that she would ever really belong anywhere.

But what she *knew* was that these huge, tumultuous, compelling emotions for him had grown, nonstop. She felt them every second she was with him. The pounding pulse. The electric current simmering under the surface. The awareness that she was female to her toes. Something about Cash brought her to life the way nothing and no one else ever had.

And in her heart, she knew she'd never feel those things again—not without him. She had no fear that life would end when she left Cash. But it would never be the same. Either she seized—and savored—this moment. Or it would be gone.

Attacking him was right.

She knew it immediately.

Everything about him applauded her choice. Just kissing him ignited her most forbidden fantasies. His taste was so distinctive…the taste of longing, the wine of desire, the whole-macho-male flavor that so specifically belonged to Cash, the part that made her…worry. Her nerves had always bubbled around his maleness, the same way a pricey Persian could instinctively sense a vagabond tomcat in the neighborhood, or the way moms locked their daughters away from certain boys. Females had a self-preservation instinct for trouble. And Cash was bad trouble for her, she'd known it from the first instant she met him.

He could break her heart.

That was part of the trouble.

She'd never be the same if they made love.

That was another frightening dimension to the trouble.

Right now, this moment, she wanted to be with him and didn't care how much she was hurt later. And that was the worst trouble of all.

But oh, he tasted rich and sexy and dangerous. His eyes

flashed on hers, as dark as a wolf's at night. She brushed his hair through her fingers, feeling the thick, wiry texture, hers to touch, hers to own...at least for that moment. And that moment was all that mattered.

Temporarily he was just letting her kiss him. An amazement in itself, she mused. He wasn't so macho, her Cash. He wasn't so cocksure. In life, he was always so unshakable, so rock solid. Climbing mountains for him was a piece of cake. But when his knuckles grazed her cheek, his touch was tender and unsteady.

It was the first time Lexie understood that he was just as afraid of risk as she was. Just as lonely. Just as positive there was no one in life for him—friends and family, sure, but not the kind of someone who could take away the abyss-blackness of night and that achy kind of loneliness.

Cash was no orphan. But she recognized another orphan of the heart. Delight kicked in, spinning with each kiss, making all those fears and risks seem no more important than drizzle. That stuff was for later.

There was no one and nothing in that dark, cramped tent but the two of them.

She took outrageously wicked sips from her tongue, took tiny nips with her teeth. She sampled his neck, his mouth, his earlobe. It wasn't really her, thumbing open the buttons of his soft flannel shirt. It wasn't her, splaying her hands, sneaking those hands in to explore his muscled chest, the smooth skin, the ripple of sinew tensing and pulsing just beneath, heating for her, heating *just* for her.

And a kiss that had started out only bravely pretending suddenly turned real and hot. Another kiss that began mischievously turned wild as a wolf's cry, a wolf's heart. She lifted his wrist, coaxed his hand to cover her breast, the most brazen of all moves, since she had no breasts, never had, never would...but oh my, his touch felt so good. She felt bursting-buxom when his palm cupped her, more so when he groaned and suddenly twisted her beneath him.

Power shifted. He tipped her back, deeper into the darkness, the air mattress making a rubbing, aching sound when he leveled her flat, and then his wet tongue was suddenly on her nipples, laving a silken path between the soft slopes and crevice between. Somehow her bra straps became all tangled up with his flannel shirt and her arms and her silk sweater, but then Cash seemed to have an outstanding solution for that.

Within seconds, all those clothes were whooshed off her and hurled heaven-knows-where.

Like a slap, the chilled night air suddenly grazed her skin intimately, brazenly, a violation—until he claimed her close again, and by that time, his shirt was gone, too. But not his pants. She wasn't sure why he left some of his clothes on, but that answer came soon enough.

He warmed her with a kiss that seeped heat from her lips to her toes, then lavished her lips with another, and another. His fingers curled her already curly hair, as if mesmerized with the texture—all her textures—in the darkness. She felt his smile of a kiss connect with her smile of a kiss, and even in the dark, she felt his eyes meeting hers, talking to hers. He wanted her. He was trying to go slower, be more patient. He was worried about pleasing her, worried this was right for her. She felt his worry, his taut effort at control, because his hands were shaking with it.

And his shaking hands made her fingers fumble for his jeans. Desire fired in his eyes like a flash of hot lightning. His hands skimmed her, up and down, claiming her, up and down. His lips dipped, not strolling kisses on her skin now but kisses that deliberately incited need and fueled hungers. Suddenly his kisses burned like hot liquid chocolate and need was a fury.

"Hurry," she whispered.

Maybe hurry was just what he wanted to hear but that slight interruption unfortunately seemed to give him a second and a half to think. "We're going awfully fast."

"You think? I figured this was just first gear." She touched his face. His neck. Felt his hard, hot body moving against hers restlessly, helplessly, as if he just couldn't stop touching her. Nor could she stop her edgy movements against him, for the same reason. "I don't know how you feel about wagers—"

"No. Don't worry, love. I'd never gamble with you or a child. I brought protection, I admit, because I was hoping—"

"I didn't mean that kind of wager. I'd never gamble with a child's life, either, Cash. This is something else, a private bet that I was thinking of making between you and me."

"Okay...so what's this bet?"

"What do you think are the odds that I can open your zipper with my teeth?"

He sucked in a rasp of a breath. "Okay. That's it. Believe me, if you're looking for trouble you just found it."

She hoped so. It seemed to Lexie that she'd been practicing denial forever. Denying that she had needs. Denying her yearning to belong. Denying, from the first day she'd arrived here, how much Cash could mean to her.

But the time for denial was done. The truth was all coming out. This second, this instant. This night. She wanted every second, every instant of this night—with him. She wasn't innocent, but there was no man who'd changed her before. She knew he could.

She knew he would.

His hands skimmed, rubbed, kneaded, teased. His fingers were ruthless, his touch stunningly skilled. In her head, she heard a silver wind, saw a thousand stars, experienced a maze of colors everywhere he touched. The night became a cascade of scents and sounds and textures that all connected to him. He stroked down her sides, her breasts, the length of her spare body, making her knees buck and bolt, wanting him closer. Wanting him naked. Wanting him inside her.

Now.

The dark heaviness building in her belly started to ache like flu. It wasn't fun anymore. Her fingertips scored his back. "No more playing," she growled.

"We haven't even started," he corrected her.

"I want you."

"I want you, too. More than I ever remember wanting or needing a woman. Only you, Lex. I've never felt this fire, not this kind of fire, for anyone but you."

"Then…take me."

"We'll take each other, I promise. But I need to please you, Lex. I need this right for you. Let me…"

He wreathed a necklace of diamond-precious kisses under her chin, in the hollow of her throat. Her heart misted. No one had ever touched her with such wonder, with such reverence. No one had ever shared the nakedness of loneliness or need with her this way. She hadn't known it could be shared with another human being. He gave her gifts, the heady feeling of beauty, the joyful exuberance of lust, the silken ropes of shared honesty…giving and giving and giving—at least until the heat sucked him under, too. There was a reason she'd been into denial all these years, she discovered. An outstanding reason that she'd been afraid of this.

Afraid of him.

Her hips lifted and her calves pedaling up, trying to cuddle around him, to rope down and in. He was already there, his gaze fierce and savage, as he cupped her bottom tighter to him and then drove in, claiming, driving, plunging deep and hard. A cry hissed from her lips, the sound as pagan as the night. He hurt her, but there'd never been this good a hurt. A kiss from her turned into a bite, warm, wet, sharp.

She smelled the spice of sweat, his, hers, the sheen on their flesh glowing like pearls.

When had the crisp, cool night turned so hot?

When had the darkness filled up with the light in his eyes, the fire in his kisses?

"Cash. Cash...I need something. Something's wrong. I can't—"

"I know." Again he arched against her, high and hard, plunging again, starting a rhythm that was older than music, a drumroll in her blood that was wildly familiar, the ancient calls of a jazz flute and its mate. She knew this man.

Somehow she'd always known him. He was the one person who could dent her personal darkness. Who somehow made the difference. Who touched her the way she had no idea a woman could be touched. Inside, outside. Making pain pretty, and soft touches fierce, and rough touches sweet, and everything he did—everything—only making her climb higher and higher.

"With me, Lexie. *With* me." She wasn't sure if he was asking her or making her a promise. It didn't matter. She *was* with him, soaring off the same cliff, flying toward a rapture that belonged to them both, and only to them. They touched gold, shuddered with the wonder of it. She cried out, then he did.

Moments passed. Eternities. Aftershocks finally quieted, gasping breaths finally slowed and eased.

Eventually, when Cash regained some strength again, he lifted his head to look at her...and she saw his dark, polished eyes. Stunned with shock, gleaming with wonder.

And she thought, I don't care what happens to me, to us. She knew better than to expect a future. No problems had disappeared, no circumstances in their lives had changed because of making love. But *she* had changed. She felt richer, more whole. Loving him was worth the hurt she knew was coming later.

Lexie refused to doubt that.

Ten

Eventually he was bound to start breathing normally again.

A guy didn't die from making love. Cash knew that. Maybe it had been a long, long time since he'd had earth-shattering sex—come to think of it, maybe never. But he could feel the cool air brushing his hot skin like a blessing, smell the tangy greens of the spring night, feel the bunched sleeping bag beneath them. Reality was still functioning. Eventually a guy always quit feeling like a shipwreck and was able to move again. Breathe again. Think again.

When Lexie snuggled her cheek into the hollow of his shoulder, Cash closed his eyes and thought: well, maybe not. Who the hell needed to think, anyway?

He'd known from day one she was trouble. He'd just never dreamed she'd be this much stupendous, terrific trouble.

When she stirred against him again, he automatically started stroking her neck and back. Light strokes. Nothing to waken or arouse her. Just a caress to keep in touch, because he was damn sure he'd have died if he had to stop touching her—even for a second.

This was *it,* he mused. Truth to tell, Cash never expected or planned to find *it* with a woman. But making love with Lexie had affirmed what he'd already suspected. There was no way in hell he was giving her up. All the practical obstacles were still there—her city life-style, her work. But surely they could find some compromise so they could live together, because she was far too much a part of his heart. And Sammy's.

When she sighed against him, he cradled her even more snugly and murmured, "Are we cold?"

"Was that a trick question? I don't even know what day it is, McKay, so don't ask me any more tough questions for a little while."

He chuckled. An owl hooted in the woods. Moonlight streamed through the tent opening in a pale patch of silver. "We sound just a tiny bit…wasted," he said delicately.

"We're never moving again, as long as we live," she added.

"Trust me, I wasn't going to suggest a *big* move. But if you'd let me shift you over, just a little, then I could unzip the sleeping bag and—"

"Forget it. You stay exactly where you are. And don't try giving me any arguments."

The way she clutched him was most satisfying. The way her lips took a bossy nip out of his neck was even more inspiring. "Um, Tiger…that's not the hardest order in town to follow. You've been teasing all this time about not having any athletic ability, but I think we finally found your sport. In fact, I think we discovered a sport that you have heretofore unrecognized Olympic talent."

"You're giving *me* credit for what just happened?"

"Well, hell. I'll take all the credit if you want. But since you're the one who put me in a near coma, I figure I should at least acknowledge that you're the most beautiful, most dangerous, most incredible lover I've ever imagined.''

Her head lifted in the darkness. Soft eyes roamed his face, as shy as the shadows. Maybe she wasn't using that petrifying ''love'' word yet, but he could feel it, see it, sense it in every movement she made. ''Not that your credibility is a question with me, McKay. You have an extraordinary amount of integrity. And I trust you. But—''

''I had a bad feeling there was a 'but' coming.''

''—But your claim of being in a near comatose state seems a little iffy. Considering that I can feel gigantic signs of life stirring against my thigh.''

''Gigantic?''

''Oh, dear. I should have known that the slightest compliment would go to your head. Heavens. I had no idea that the dead could rise like that. You *can't* be in the mood again this soon.''

Well, he hadn't been, until she started wiggling and squirming and teasing him. ''Me? Hey, I was gonna be a gentleman and roll over and go to sleep, start snoring on you like any decent, normal male human being. But then you started flaunting that body of yours at me again—''

''*Me?* Flaunting? Why, you…why, you—'' When she couldn't seem to come up with an insult vile enough to describe his character, she reached up and kissed him. Or he reached down and plucked a fat, wet, sweet kiss from her. Who started the devilment seemed a moot issue. Within seconds they were both laughing.

Cash stopped laughing first, about the same instant he realized their play was evolving into lovemaking. He'd cared the first time was good for her, but this time he felt as if his life depended on making this right for Lexie. He wanted this chance. He needed it. If a bear had ambled up to their tent, he doubted he'd have noticed or cared.

When a man had a mission, it took his utmost concentration. He wanted no inch on her body that didn't have his stamp, his kiss, his appreciation connected to it. Desire and desperation both started drumming in his pulse with an insistent, building beat. Maybe, when he was ninety, he'd be able to see some humor in the irony of Cashner Aaron Mc-Kay feeling sucked under with fear. He'd avoided commitment so successfully all these years—only to fall for the one woman in the universe who was extra impossible to both woo and win.

Lexie was leaving in less than two weeks. That ticking clock added passion to every kiss, urgency to every touch, a lightning surge of hope for every sigh and groan he earned from her.

He couldn't make Lexie want to stay. He knew that. He also knew that she thought of this land as a wilderness, not a paradise. Cash could compromise. Could move. But not for the wrong reasons. Somehow, back when he'd had an orphan suddenly sprung on him, it seemed right to come here. Sammy was a wounded little kid, and Cash wanted to raise him with the right values, in a place that was healing and renewing. He'd never held onto a buck back in his business days, but he'd known how to bring in a decent salary. This mattered more…and Cash kept thinking, it could for Lexie, too. She needed healing, too. She needed a place to belong.

Yet Cash knew the odds of his winning her were pit low. Maybe she was an orphan, but she wasn't his orphan. And she was leaving in less than two weeks unless something drastic changed to make her rethink what she wanted from life.

Maybe loving the wits right out of her was a less than honorable thing to do. But he was fighting for both himself and Sammy. The ends were just going to have to justify the means.

* * *

"Wait a minute, Cash. Tell me again. I still don't unner-stand how you and Lexie got locked in the library after lunch."

"Well, I don't really know, sport. I must have acciden-tally flipped the latch when I went in there, so that I didn't realize it was locked." Typically during their sacred dad-and-son time after dinner, Cash stashed in an easy chair with his feet cocked on the coffee table. And Sammy's favorite posture for discussing life was upside down on the couch, with his stocking feet up on the wall—although one sock, Cash noted, had a hole in the big toe.

"But there's no way to accidentally flip the latch. I know, 'cause I went up and tried before dinner. It's hard to lock that door. Almost impossible. There's a mystery around here," Sammy said darkly.

Cash tugged at the throat of his shirt. He loved these daily times with Sammy. Usually. "I don't think you need to worry about it."

"I'm not *worried*. I just think it's weird that we're having this sudden problem with locks. Like the way you and Lexie got locked in the massage room two days ago. That's twice where you guys got locked together—"

Again, Cash tugged at the shirt collar, but he still couldn't seem to give his neck any more breathing room. Conducting a love affair with a lot of people around was challenging. Conducting a spontaneous love affair with a young boy around—even when said young boy had five million care-takers all over the Sam Hill place—was damn near impos-sible. Hoping to distract him, Cash tried another subject. "Hey, you haven't told me how Martha and the puppies are doing today."

"I think we should talk some more about Lexie getting locked in places. You know, Cash, I don't think she's real smart. I think she should stay with us a while longer. Like another month. She needs a lot of lessons on how to be safe. Like the kind we could teach her. I don't think she should go back to the city for a long time.''

Neither did Cash, and the attachment Sammy had formed for Lexie stripped a new tear out of his heart. No matter what happened, Sammy's fondness for Lexie was a good thing. Cash had quit worrying about that. Every minute they were together, Lexie seemed to give the kid confidence and perspective that a male could never have offered him. But without question, Sammy *was* going to feel the bite if—when—Lexie took off.

''She's got a job she can't just leave, Sam. No matter what, she's got stuff to take care of. We talked about that before. And just because she has to leave doesn't mean she'll never come back,'' Cash said with careful tact, but somehow he couldn't sit and talk about this. His boots were already swinging for the floor, his shoulders hunching in tense knots. After dinner was historically the time Sammy always hit him with touchy subjects.

But in this case, Lexie was already a painfully touchy subject for him. Another five days had passed since the night they'd camped out and made love. They'd had an extraordinary week together, not just having fun, but talking, becoming close. *Really* close. Heart close, gut close. Lexie gave and gave and gave. She came into his arms with a spirit of fun and a powder keg of passion both. She never held anything back, took him out every time. There's no way that woman was afraid of loving.

But she was damn well afraid of something, because no matter how often she willingly came into his arms, long before she'd scooted back to her own bed. She never let on that a short-term affair wasn't just her cup of tea. She never suggested growing the least attached to Silver Mountain. She never hinted there was even a prayer she might consider staying.

Sammy finally tired of standing on his head, and red-faced, draped himself over the couch edge instead. "How many of the puppies do you think we should keep?" he asked innocently.

"Nice try. But I thought we *clearly* agreed that we were going to give them away when they were six weeks old."

"Now come on, Cash," Sammy wheedled. "You're the only one who agreed. Not me. And I think the puppies'd be lonely without me. What if Martha took off? Then I'd be the only parent they had."

More touchy subjects. But then that's why Cash had adopted Martha, so Cash could see that all moms didn't take off on their children. "Are you having a good time watching Martha being a mom?"

"Oh, yeah. I think it's way cool, the way she moves 'em around and hides 'em to keep them safe. Even though there aren't any wolves or coyotes in the house and there's really no reason to move them."

"But it's a way you can see how much she loves them, right?"

"Yeah, right. And she licks 'em all the time. They're not even dirty and she's licking 'em. And she growls when strangers come around. That's weird, huh?"

"What's weird?" Cash asked.

"You know. How Martha has a cow when strangers try to look at her babies. My mom felt 'xactly the other way. She left me like she didn't care who I was with."

"Oh, no, sport. She cared. She knew you'd be with me, and she knew I loved you like a son from the day you were born." Cash wasn't leaving him any room for doubts on that score.

"But that's how you are. What I was talking about was how women are. Like Martha and my mom. And Martha, she thinks all the time about protecting her babies. But Mom,

I don't think she even thinks about protecting me. But maybe human moms and animal moms are different, huh?''

"I think everybody tries to do the best they can. Sometimes they just make choices that aren't right. But it's not because they're not trying."

This effort at philosophy flew over Sammy's head. Or else he ignored it. He pointed a finger at Cash, getting back to his point. "Pers'nally, I think Lexie would kill anyone who came near *her* babies."

"Um, kill is a pretty strong word, slugger."

"Yeah, and she's a little person, besides. And clumsy, too. But all the same, when we're out walking, if she hears a sound, she jumps in front of me. She really makes me laugh. Like she could protect me from a bear or something. But you know what? I think Lexie needs a puppy, too."

"You've got no end of interesting ideas tonight, don't yo—'' Cash's head automatically swiveled around when he heard the phone jangle.

"I'll get it, I'll get it!" Even at eight o'clock at night, Sammy still had energy to burn. He leaped over the back of the couch, hurtled over the ottoman and galloped for the receiver. "Hello, it's the McKay residence. Can I help you?—that is, unless you're a telemarketer, in which case I'm gonna get my dad and you're gonna be real, real sorry you called our number."

Cash winced. Well, at least the kid remembered *some* of the phone manners he'd been taught. And it was time to get this household settled down and straightened up. He scooped up some glasses and socks and marbles—for starters—but he stayed close enough to half-listen to Sammy just in case the phone call was business.

Within moments, he realized the call wasn't business— but it was something serious. Sammy straightened up like a soldier and his voice turned earnest. He spilled out some information that couldn't possibly make sense to any caller, but he was obviously trying to help. "Yeah, she's here in the lodge. Don't you worry. I'll get her right away. It'll take a minute, because she moved in the room down the hall when the puppies were born, and I have to run down there and knock. So don't hang up, okay? Don't hang up. I'll get her, I promise."

Something was so wrong in Sammy's tone that Cash was already striding to take the receiver when Sammy let it clatter on the table.

"I have to find Lexie right away. It's a girl on the phone. And she's crying. And she says she's Lexie's sister. So I gotta go get her, okay?"

"Okay, sport—you can run faster than I can. But if she isn't in her room, come back immediately to tell me, all right? Then we'll do whatever we have to do to track her down."

Talk about your complete goofballs.

A few minutes earlier, Lexie had ambled into her bedroom after dinner and pushed off her shoes. There was nothing odd about that. She couldn't pinpoint the precise moment the goofball thing had kicked in...but suddenly she realized that she was lying flat on the bed, staring at the plank-board ceiling, humming old, wicked rock and roll and hugging herself.

The emotion dancing through her whole system—mind and body—seemed a remarkable one. Happiness. Plain old, silly old, who'd-a-believed-it, delirious happiness.

All right, she was living out a dream. She admitted it. She didn't expect the spell to last—she admitted that, too. But the instant she squeezed her eyes closed, images dawdled and sauntered through her mind again. Cash, chasing her into the library after lunch, and seducing her right there between the sunlit bookcases. Her, cornering him in the massage room a couple of days ago, and seducing him right there on that itty-bitty narrow table. Yesterday afternoon, playing hide-and-seek in the woods—with neither of them hiding very hard—and both of them having to sneak back into the lodge covered with dirt and damp spring leaves.

And it wasn't just sex. Making love was a marvel that just kept getting wilder and more wonderful, but other times were just as magical. Romping with both Sammy and Cash in the long grassy field that rolled down to the creek. The three of them nestled on the floor with Martha's puppies....

With a sign, Lexie's eyes flashed open. She told herself to get up, move, quit mooning around. She'd never felt loved before—not the way Cash made her feel. She'd never loved anyone else the fierce, huge, wondrous way that she loved him.

She wasn't counting on it to last.

She *wasn't*.

There was nothing wrong with loving him—or Sammy— as long as she was the only one risking getting hurt. She'd known that making love with Cash would change her life, change her. She'd known he was different than any other man who'd ever been in her life. And she'd known from day one that she couldn't possibly fit in at Silver Mountain for long. So what? So the dream would be over and the spell broken and her heart was going to splinter. She knew that.

And didn't give a damn.

Every moment with both of them was worth it. Was worth everything. She wouldn't trade a second of these days and weeks with the McKays for all the tea in...but that thought suddenly shunted off when someone rapped on her door.

Swiftly she jerked to a sitting position and scooched off the bed. "Just a second, I'm coming!" Her downstairs room was more spacious than the one Martha had usurped as a birthing center. Her eyes darted over the chestnut plank floor, searching under the Lincoln rocker and under the Federal bureau and by the long bed chest for her shoes—and when she couldn't find them, decided she didn't need them anyway. She pushed a hand through her hair, checked to make sure her blouse was buttoned and her slacks zipped, then zigzagged across a fallen coat and a couple of books and a footstool toward the door.

None of that took her more than seconds, yet still, someone pounded several more times on the door. "Lexie! It's *me*. I need you!"

That was enough to make her vault the last foot and yank the door open lickety split. "I was coming, Sammy, it's just that I…" She saw Martha next to Sammy, but for once the mama dog didn't get attention from either of them. All Lexie could focus on was the expression on the boy's face. "Sweetheart, what's wrong?"

"Your sister. She's on the phone. Come on in our living room. She's all upset, Lexie, and I promised I'd get you—"

"And you did. Did she say her name, Sammy? Because I've got a couple of sisters." She left the door gaping open as they both pelted toward Cash's apartments. Even with both of them hustling, though, her hand instinctively dropped to Sammy's shoulders to give him a reassuring squeeze. It was all she could do not to kiss the darling. Yeah, she was worried about whatever the family problem was, but Sammy had one of Those Looks in his eyes—he was a big man at the moment, feeling important, proud to be a hero, to be the one to fetch her. "I can't thank you enough for coming to find me."

Those skinny shoulders swelled another five feet. "Yeah, well, me and Cash woulda torn apart the whole lodge to find you, if we had to. We'd never have let you down. Cash! I got her, I got her! It's that phone, over by the couch…."

She saw. And she quickly aimed for the phone, but it was Cash filling her eyes, Cash filling her mind, when she tripped over a soccer ball and then accidentally sent a glass teetering from the lamp table.

"Whatever it is, try to take it easy, I'll help," Cash mouthed when she finally managed to grab the receiver. He tried to herd Sammy out of sight and hearing range, but Sammy clearly didn't want to leave her. And Cash might have been trying to give her some privacy, but he was obviously concerned something serious had happened to a family member of hers, too, and didn't want to stray too far.

At dinner, she distinctly remembered that stockinged foot of Cash's climbing her leg under the table, teasing, flirting...and her stockinged foot had been flirting up his muscular leg, no differently. That play was part of who they were together, but now, she saw the steadfast concern in his eyes. Cash's brand of rock solid caring, being there for those he loved—the real reason she'd fallen so hopefully in love with him.

Right then, though, she had her sister to deal with. "Okay, Freda, just calm down...yes, of course I remember talking about the 'dogs of the Dow.' I can't believe you did that. You, of all people..."

Cash put a glass of water in her hand. Sammy showed up with a towel to pretend to mop up whatever was in the first spilled glass. Both male eyes tracked her expressions until she could hardly think.

"Of course I understand sudden expenses, Freda. But that's exactly why I can't believe that you took this kind of financial risk to begin with. No, quit crying, sis, I promise, this is the easiest thing to fix on the planet. Everything's going to be fine."

Yet nothing was fine. Her ears were suddenly ringing, her stomach lurching uneasily. Lexie couldn't make sense of the sudden assault of dizzying sensations. Naturally she felt badly that her sister was upset, but she felt thrilled that Freda had called her for help.

Probably it was always going to be her worst nightmare, to know someone she loved was hurting and feeling impo-

tent to help them. This was nothing like the situation that
happened to her parents, of course, but Freda was in a spot
of trouble. And of all Lexie's adoptive sisters, Freda was
not only especially loving, but she was also blond and beautiful and statuesque—and so athletically talented that she had
a zillion sports trophies. Lexie had always felt like such a
clumsy dolt next to her adoptive family, and especially
Freda. This was the first time her sister had ever needed her.
And even more to the point, Lexie was uniquely qualified
to help her.

"...No, you silly. This is nothing. I'll just buy the 'dog'
stocks from you...." In spite of her roiling stomach, Lexie
swiftly calculated. "...Say, at nine percent, so you won't
have to worry about suffering such a loss—no, no, stop worrying about it. But don't do this again, all right? If you want
to invest, talk to me first. The 'dogs of the Dow' were never
going to be a good idea for you—okay, okay. I love you,
too. Stop worrying, stop even thinking about this, sis...."

It was all good, the call with her sister. Hearing Freda's
voice. Knowing that she really was helping her. So there
was no explaining why Lexie's heart kept sinking down a
dark, deep well. She looked at Cash and could feel panic
balling in her stomach. Tears welling and stinging in her
eyes. Her pulse suddenly pumping, thumping, at a bazillion
miles an hour.

"Okay, talk to you soon, Freda...I'll have this taken care
of by tomorrow. I'll call you then." Lexie saw Cash suddenly frown, suddenly bolt toward her. She'd just managed
to hang up the phone before she felt his big, calm hand at
the back of her neck, urging her to put her head between
her knees.

"Cash! What's wrong with our Lexie? What's wrong,
what's wrong?"

She heard Sammy's frantic voice, but mostly she heard
Cash's. His tone was gentle and quiet, as soothing as a long,

golden sip of old brandy. "Just breathe slow and easy, love. Don't think. Don't talk. Just try to breathe in, breathe out. Sammy, she's fine. Or she's going to be fine. It would help her if you and me could be real quiet for a few minutes, okay?"

"I'm fine," she tried to say, but it wasn't true. When he called her "love"—and in front of Sammy—her heart slammed even harder. And Cash hunched down, trying to get down to eye level with her so he could study her face. His hand was still on her back, soothing, soothing, communicating reassurance and trust. The trust thing almost struck her sense of humor.

Cash didn't need to promise her trust. She already knew she could trust him to the nth degree. He was that kind of man—and for damn sure, that kind of lover. Ironically her faith in his integrity only seemed to intensify the anxiety attack symptoms.

"Sammy," Cash continued calmly, "Keegan said that he'd be baking all kinds of things tonight, pies, cookies and all…if you go in the kitchen, I know he'll let you help. You can even stay up—"

Sammy wasn't fooled by the bribe. "I don't want to leave Lexie."

"I'll take care of Lexie."

"Cash." Lexie lifted her swimming head. "Sammy's going to worry if he can't see I'm okay. Sammy, see? I just got dizzy for a second. I'm happy. I'm healthy." She offered him a five-hundred-volt smile. Or her best faked high-voltage one. "See? I just need to sit still for a second, that's all."

"No. Something was wrong." Sammy hunkered down on the couch next to her, squishing-close. "And it was something about your sister, right? Something about puppies?"

"Puppies?"

"Yeah. You were talking about dogs. I heard you. Cash, I *know* you can make Lexie tell us what was wrong—"

Lexie scrubbed her forehead. She had to fix this. Fast. Sammy already had the worrisome idea that women weren't dependable...that women took off when there was a problem. She couldn't have him thinking that about her. Again she forced a smile. And forced her annoying, exasperating, racing pulse to—damnation!—slow down.

"I was talking with my sister about stocks, Sammy. But I'm afraid if I explain, I'll just bore you to death—"

"I won't be bored. And Cash won't be bored. We wanna hear about these dogs."

Her palms were still damp with nerves, her mind lightheaded. But she didn't mind explaining her sister's problem. It wasn't that she wanted to bore her McKay boys, but talking about something so basic to her gave Lexie some time to get past this mortifying anxiety attack.

"The 'dogs of the Dow,' honey, is just a phrase to describe the worst performing stocks in the market. And some people specifically love to gamble on the dogs—meaning they like to invest in the four or five worst of those stocks— and hold them for a year. Historically, the dogs report a pretty solid nineteen percent return for the money. But the way that works, is that you only hold those stocks for a year, then get rid of them, then pick up the next year's dogs. You get me?"

"Cripes, no," Sammy said disgustedly.

"Well, I do," Cash said. "Just go on, Lex. I'll explain to Sammy later whatever he doesn't get."

"Okay. Well, my sister Freda, she's wonderful, and really bright, but I'm afraid she's not cool with numbers. It's the one thing in the family that I *am* good at. Figures. Money. And sometime she must have heard me talking about the 'dogs of the Dow' and thought, wow, she wanted that nineteen percent—"

"Uh-huh." Again, Cash urged a sip of water on her, and then removed the glass before she could spill it.

"Only Freda, as smart as she is, doesn't quite get how stocks work. And normally she makes a good living, but a bunch of things hit her at once—her washing machine died, and then her car. So she needed some savings right away, but the thing was, she'd invested in the dogs, and she was going to lose a bundle if she pulled out now...."

"I get it, I get it."

"There was no real reason for her to be so shook up. I think she was just embarrassed. And afraid she was going to lose her hard-earned money." Cash's hand was so cool, so soothing, that she closed her eyes for a second. "But there was no fear of that. I'll buy the stocks from her, and give her the profit for the weeks she held them. She'll have the cash to make her down payment on another car. And she won't do this again. Problem solved. Everything's fine."

Sammy pushed at her knee, his expression still worried. "But then, if it's all so easy, how come you got so upset, Lexie?"

Because the dream was over.

The spell was broken.

Cash's Dow was never going to fit with her Jones. And that wasn't news—Lexie had known that all along—but her sister calling had punched that reality right in her stomach. And it hurt.

Money was the kind of problem she knew how to fix. There was nothing she could do here. She couldn't help Cash or Sammy, nor could she possibly fit in. Climbing mountains wasn't her. Wearing sloppy old Nikes wasn't her. Cavorting with her lover, day and night, maybe that *was* her...but Cash had a son. A son he adored. And any woman in Cash's life had to be right for Sammy or there was no spell, no magic, no nothing.

There was only one person she'd been kidding, to allow

herself to fall so deeply, to become so hugely involved in their lives. Herself. She'd just hoped to matter to someone sometime. Hoped to make a difference in someone's life. But it was foolish for her to count on fitting in Sammy's—much less in Cash's—when she knew better and had always known better.

It was time to go home. To get away. Before she risked Cash realizing how deeply she'd fallen in love with him.

Eleven

Cash bent down to tuck in the blanket. "Now, I know you're so big you don't need a good-night hug any more, sport, but it's one of those nights I could use one…if you don't mind."

"Nah. It's okay, as long as it's just for you." Sammy's skinny arms roped around his neck and squeezed tight. "You're gonna talk to Lexie, aren't you?"

"Yup. I'll sit with her a while, and then walk her back to her room, make sure she's okay." When Cash straightened up, he patted the pager hooked to his belt. "If you need me, you know you can get me in a few seconds flat. And I won't be any further than down the hall."

"What, you think I'm still a baby? I don't need you." Sammy's tone reeked disgust, but then he hesitated. "You gotta find out why she was so upset, okay?"

"I'll try."

"It wasn't her sister. She didn't even sound upset about her sister. She sounded glad her sister called."

"That's what I thought, too."

"Cash? I gotta tell you something else."

"Okay, I'm here." At the door, he flicked off the overhead and then waited. As much as he wanted to hustle back to Lexie and make sure she was over that panic attack, he'd never hurried anything about Sammy's bedtime or ever wanted the kid to think he wasn't Cash's first priority.

Finally Sammy squirmed out what was on his mind. "I think she's the one for us." He added slowly, "My mom...she isn't coming back for me, you know."

One of these years, the damn kid was going to make his heart break. "I'm afraid she isn't likely to come home to stay, either," he said quietly.

"Yeah, well, I knew that ages ago, really. I just wasn't sure if you did. Mom doesn't want me. That's just the way it is. But all this time, I didn't want a mom, either. I didn't want anybody but you and me. The real truth of the matter is, I don't have a lot of use for women. Any more than you do. Only now..."

"What, son?"

The kid's voice was softer than a whisper. "I want her to stay. Lexie. For you. But just a little bit...for me, too. And I know she wouldn't stay, not for somebody who doesn't matter much like me, but maybe if you asked her...she might." He added swiftly, "Not that I care too much."

"Samuel McKay, you matter," Cash said fiercely. So much that sometimes he wanted to wring his sister's neck, for so carelessly shredding the boy's sense of self-worth. So much that sometimes the damn kid made his whole heart ache. "I'm going to tell you a secret, though. Man-to-man."

"Oh, good. I like it when we share man-to-man secrets, Cash."

"I know you do. And this is the secret. I care about Lexie. A lot. But everybody's looking for something, Sammy. And I don't know that what Lexie needs in her life, she can find in Idaho. Even if she loves the two of us. Even if she really cares. It doesn't mean she can stay, slugger, and I'll be damned if I'll promise you otherwise.''

"Don't swear, Cash.''

"Hell. I didn't mean to.'' Cash swiped his jaw.

"And I know all that, anyway. That's how Mom is. She needs something. Only it isn't me. It's never me. So I already know how that goes. But I just wanted you to know, that it's okay if you get close with Lexie. She's okay with me. That's all I wanted you to know. I'm not gonna quit being against women, for Pete's sake. Just her. She's the 'xception. I think she could be the 'xception for you, too.''

"Okay.'' Cash cleared his throat. "I'm glad we got that stuff said. I appreciate your being willing to talk man-to-man with me.''

"Yeah, me, too. Only let's not do it too often, okay? All this talking can wear a guy out. Just go fix Lexie, all right?''

As if he had a magic pill to make everything right for Lex. And the kid's faith weighed on Cash's shoulders as he strode back into the living room.

She was still there. Not sitting on the couch anymore, though. Now she was standing at the window, her back to him, staring out at the velvet spring night, her arms huddled around her chest...her stocking foot tapping silently, as if antsy to leave. A wave of love gushed through Cash so fast and hard that he felt sucked under its ocean current, buffeted to somewhere out of his control and unfamiliar.

It was the curl of springy hairs at her nape. And that skinny little fanny. And the pride in her, in the independent tilt to her shoulders, in the lonely way she stood. When she heard his footsteps, she whirled around with the passion of fire in her eyes—fire for him.

He saw the fire.

And he saw her mask it.

"I'll say good night. I almost left when you were putting

Sammy to bed, but I didn't want to just take off without saying anything.''

"I figured you'd be beat. But I'll walk you down the hall.'' She looked better, he thought. A little color brushed high on her cheeks. The frantic anxiety in her movements had eased up. But she ambled next to him down the hall, not looking at him, stiff as a board.

He didn't figure she'd willingly say anything where anyone in the lodge could pass by, but they reached her room in moments. She'd left the door gaping open, and he followed her in.

Dusk had fallen, heavy now, but she made no move to turn on any lights and neither did Cash. He hoped the darkness might make it easier for her to talk with him. "Lex...I don't understand what happened. What caused that panic attack?''

He saw her throw up her hands in the silhouette of the window. "I don't know. Honestly. I tried to tell you before, sometimes those attacks just seem to come out of nowhere.''

"But you just mentioned yesterday that you'd been sleeping like a brick, no more insomnia. And you hadn't had one of those panic things in ages now, either.''

"Yeah. Silver Mountain's helped me shake both problems, for real. You were right about these mountains having magic. I must have been a little off tonight, that's all.'' She lifted a smile for him—a smile pale as moonlight.

He jammed a boot forward. "I want to help, love. Just tell me how.''

There. The steel melted from her shoulders right now. "Aw, McKay. Being in your life these last three weeks was worth gold to me. More gold than I can even try to tell you. You've already helped me more than anyone I can remember.''

Hell. The words were real sweet, but they sounded like

the prelude to a goodbye to him. Alarm knifed through his nerves. "Lexie. I *love* you."

She didn't come closer. She didn't hesitate to respond for even a second, either. "God knows, I love you, too. I'd do anything for you. And Sammy. I feel like you're more part of my life than my own heartbeat."

He caught another moonlit smile from her. The smile seemed real, just as real as her words, but something in her eyes was scaring the stuffing right out of him.

"Cash...I'm glad you walked me back here, because I didn't want to risk Sammy overhearing this, but I wanted to tell you—I'm sorry. I know I frightened Sammy with that anxiety attack. I never meant for him to see me acting like such a goose."

"You're not a goose." A hot puddle of nerves seemed to settle in his stomach, and contrarily, made him short of breath. "Lexie?"

"What?"

"Lexie..." That time he got her name out, before that hot puddle of nerves tried to choke him up again.

"What?" she repeated.

"Would you consider...marrying me?" The words came out as crusty as rust scraped from an old barrel. He'd just never used those words before. Not paired together with a question hovering at the end like a bullet hanging out of a gun.

And when Lexie went still and didn't instantly answer him, he bumbled in with more words. Nonstop words. Anything to prevent her from having the chance to say no. "I know we've only known each other a month. But we've seen each other every day, all day. It's not like city life where people date but never have the chance to see each other in any real way at all." He gulped in a breath, and when she didn't manage to get a word in then, he forged on. "Obviously you have to go back. You've got a serious business, issues that can't be fixed or taken care of long distance. And I don't understand altogether what you do, never did, but between a modem and fax and airplanes, couldn't you really work wherever you wanted to? I'm not saying we have to be *here,* Silver Mountain, at least not all the time. But for what you do, isn't it possible to have an office in a house instead of in a steel-and-glass high-rise?''

''Cash...'' Slow now, as slow as the slide of silk, she lifted her face and started walking toward him.

Saying his name sure as hell wasn't the same thing as saying yes. ''I'm not asking you to give anything up. I'd never want you to give up your work or anything that matters to you. I'm just asking if some compromise might not open up the possibilities. I'm asking if there's any way—any wild way—you could imagine taking on one grown man and one small boy in the wilds of Idaho.''

She was still walking toward him, but all he heard was the silence. It was obvious he'd stunned her, obvious that Lexie had never expected any of this. But the silence was suddenly pounding in his ears like a jungle drum thumping out a warning about danger coming, and that was it. He couldn't take it.

In one clipped step, he was close enough to swing his arms around her. He bent his head and gave her a kiss that might as well have had her name on it...then took a kiss that pumped in every ounce of power and passion he owned. It wasn't nice, overpowering a woman. He told himself to cut it out, to give her some time.

He told himself to slow down, and for God's sake to be the honorable gentleman his grandmother had raised him to be.

Only just then, he couldn't seem to conjure up a holy damn about honor. He tasted her, and went back for more. His boot heel kicked the door shut. On the back swing he managed to have her tumbled on the bed.

All of a sudden, he couldn't think of a single thing he had to offer Lexie. Nothing he loved or did had anything to do with the life-style she was used to. So—if and when he got around to letting her answer him—she was doubtless going to have a brain and say no. He got that. But nothing was ever going to be right in his life again without her. Nothing was going to be as much fun. As much trouble. As much worry.

Everything about her had his knickers in a twist. Her nightmares and her independence, her panic attacks and her pride. That slow, sweeping smile of hers tickled his hormones, no different than the way she slouched down when she was walking to Sammy to be more on a level with the kid. He liked the way she raided Keegan's private stash of snickerdoodles in the kitchen and the way she'd baby-talked to the puppies and shrieked about spiders. He loved the way she talked to Sammy. And she got to him, because she was lonely and isolated and alone, like him, damnation, *just* like him. Then there was that other little detail. The way she kissed.

No woman in the universe could take a man out more lethally than Alexandra, not when she was in the mood, and at that precise moment, Ms. Woolf seemed to have lost all control. All that love stuff kept bubbling through his mind like champagne, the bubbles so thick he couldn't see or think through them...and all because she was kissing him back. Possibly he'd been a tad rough, throwing her on the bed.

It was her arms around him now.

And her mouth open under his kisses, tongue-to-tongue talking.

And her short leg was hitched up and wound around his thigh, drawing him to her, drawing him against her, and she was rubbing like a cat pushing against catnip. There was love in her kisses.

He *knew* there was.

Her shirt raveled off her head easily enough. Easier yet
to chase down her slacks, with a scrap of silk underpants
stripping down at the same time. He managed to pull off
one of her socks before a pillow skidded on the floor, and
the blankets suddenly bunched, and her hands in the darkness—her city-girl, pampered hands—were suddenly fram-
ing his face and stealing a kiss...a hot, wet kiss...just as
brazen as a robber near an unlocked bank vault.

Her fingers found his jeans snap. She was getting awfully
good at that. And then her hand slid down, inside. A fingertip discovered the length of him, and then her palm
cupped him in that warm, dark nest of her hand.

"Lexie—"

"Don't talk. We don't need to talk," she whispered.

"Yeah, we do," he insisted. Yet as conscious as he was
that she hadn't answered him about the marriage question,
the bigger truth was that Cash was afraid of talking. He
didn't know the words to win her. He didn't know the words
that might make a difference. He only knew how to express
how much he'd come to love her, the best way he could.

The most vulnerable way he could.

So he kissed her again...on her mouth. Down her neck.
His tongue made a damp trail between her breasts, over the
tips, under the swell, down to the navel. He knew how un-
alike they were. He knew how many compromises they had
ahead of them. He understood—exactly—how wary she'd
be of tying up with anyone like him. But he also knew everything was right with her. Laughing. Eating, reading, fighting. Differences didn't matter, not once he realized that
every second of every day was right because she was in it.

He'd hidden those feelings from her before, but now he
laid himself bare. What made them right together was her
and him at the core. It was about the dark abyss. Feeling
alone on the inside. *Being* alone on the inside—until she
flew into his life and tripped on his front porch.

He tried to tell her all of it. Everything. He whisked kisses down her leg, then back up the inside of her thigh, then tried that same path again, since it seemed to inspire a dangerously pagan response from her. In the darkness, he caught the warm, vibrant scent of her skin, the silver light in her eyes, the lightning connection he felt in her touch, in her rasping for breath and urgent pulse, slamming, slamming against him. Her skin turned hot. Damp. Her nails dug into his back, clutching, impatient.

But he didn't want this to end. Ever, if it were up to him. He rode her once with his tongue, taking her mountain climbing to exactly the heights she'd been afraid of before. She hadn't trusted him weeks before. Hell, he hadn't trusted her, either. But that was the difference in loving; she *did* trust him now and this was the only way he knew to prove it to her. He took her high, so high the air was shallow and she was gasping for breath.

Once she peaked that first time, he moved to claim her, climbing on, stroking his way in, as slowly as tenderness, but then taking her deep and high all over again. He never thought he could win her as a lover, but it was a million times more than passion or pleasure in his head. This was the only way he knew to tell her what he was willing to risk. Everything he was. Everything he wanted to be. For her, with her.

Only it just couldn't last. There was no way to stop the momentum when a rocket was soaring a thousand miles an hour. Still, he felt like he was soaring straight into her. The joy of wonder in her eyes in the darkness, in his dark heart from the inside out. It was love she shared with him. Love she gave.

When he crashed, moments later, he was both completely spent and bursting high with hope. It was no time to talk. She was as weak and beat as he was. But he pulled her close in his arms and wrapped the covers around both of them, zonking out on the same pillow with her. It was going to be all right. He knew it. He kissed her smile with his smile just before dropping off into a deep sleep.

Cash woke up in the muzzy part of dawn, disturbed by a sound he couldn't identify. Lexie was snugly wrapped around him. She'd stolen ninety percent of the pillow and ninety-five of the comforter in the night. His backside was hanging out, but it wasn't the cold that wakened him. It was...

That. The small *thwump* at the foot of the bed. When he heard the sound a second time, his eyes shot open. His vision was still bleary from lack of sleep, but then he heard another discordant sound. Panting. And although heaven knew, he and Lexie had done their share of panting during the wee hours, this just didn't sound at all the same.

He peeked over the covers.

There seemed to be, between his feet and hers, two puppies. And then another face formed in the gray predawn light at the foot of the bed—Martha's. She had another puppy in her mouth, and with another *thwump,* deposited Baby Three with the rest of her brood.

"How on *earth* did you get in here, Martha?" he snarled.

Lexie's eyes were closed, and he knew his voice had barely hit a whisper. Still, she smiled in the dawn light, as if she'd been awake for a while. "It seems that Martha and I have an understanding—even if she's the only one who understands. She goes where I go. Even if that means moving her puppies."

"And now I remember...this door was open last night, wasn't it, when we first came in?"

"Uh-huh. Get back down here and snuggle, McKay. You're letting in cold air. I'm cold."

"Not in this life, you're not," he assured her.

She chuckled. "It's way too early to flirt, you devil. Just come back down here and warm me up before I beat you."

"Good threat, Lex. I'm impressed. But unfortunately, I think I'd better get next door before the kid wakes up. Besides which—I might as well admit, I'm not one of those liberal men. There are too many bodies in this bed for me."

"Are you telling me you'd have a problem if Elle MacPherson decided to join us?" Maybe the voice was cobwebby and sticky with sleep, but her humor was definitely wide-awake.

"I hate to tell you this, love, but I'd take you over a thousand Elles." He patted her rump, then kissed a grin on the downy hair spot at her nape. "Go back to sleep. But fair warning. As soon as I catch you alone today, we're going to have a nice little terrifying talk about rings. And kids. And that really scary word—marriag—"

Her head whirled around so fast, she almost clipped him in the chin. And in spite of the foggy light, he clearly saw the look in her eyes.

Saw the fear.

Saw the color wash right out of her face.

Saw the "no" in her expression even before she had the chance to say it. Dread eclipsed his earlier hope. Damnation, he *knew* love was there. No woman had ever loved him the way she did when the lights went out or when the lights were on, for that matter. She bared her soul when they were alone together. She trusted him completely with her body.

But some part of her was still guarded, still afraid. Cash didn't know what it was, but one thing was for sure.

He was a pinch away from losing her, completely and forever, unless he could figure out what the problem was. Pronto.

Twelve

By dinner, Cash had had all he could take. All day, he'd been trying to find a place and time to talk with Lexie. And all day, he'd run into her nonstop. Naturally there'd been a crowd around for the morning exercise but right after that, he'd caught her heading into the gym with Bubba. After that, he caught her munching on a snack with Keegan, and later, romping with Martha and Sammy in the front yard. She'd squeezed his shoulder at lunch, but that was the closest she came within five of feet of him where other accidental chaperons weren't around.

When he walked into dinner and realized she wasn't there, the stress churning in his stomach added some real spikes. It wasn't like anyone *had* to honor the dinner hour. The kitchen was always open. People could eat whenever they wanted. Still, Cash would have to be a prize dolt not to realize the obvious. Lexie didn't want to be around him.

He pushed the food around his plate all through dinner, his gaze half peeled on the door. She never showed.

Even a prize-dolt could figure out what was wrong. He should have waited before asking her the Major Marriage question. He also should have staged something romantic instead of being so blasted honest—any guy knew that being blunt and honest was stupid with a woman. More to the point, it was just too soon. Something big had always been bothering Lexie—that same "something" that troubled her long before she came to Silver Mountain and that caused her insomnia and panic attack problems to start with.

The problem was, that he had no time. He was pretty sure he knew what that Serious Something was, but Lexie was leaving in a matter of days now. And although in principle, he figured he'd asked the petrifying marriage question too fast, he was drop-sure she loved him, drop-sure he adored her beyond all reason. He wasn't really afraid they couldn't untangle the rest, as long as the love thing was absolutely right. Only Lexie obviously wasn't on that absolute track. And right now, his only choice was determining how to recoup from a woman running ninety miles an hour in any direction he wasn't.

He pick-and-pecked through dinner, got Sammy settled with Keegan and a board game at the kitchen table. By then it was dusk, and Cash slipped out the back door, determined to get some think-time in the fresh air. He couldn't afford to make any more mistakes.

Outside, it was buttery quiet and still, shadows tiptoeing between the trees as the day started falling. He walked like a machine, putting one boot in front of the other, with her face on his mind, on his heart. He told himself it was never over until the fat lady sung. So Lexie wasn't ready. So she had to go back to the city. So? It wasn't like all doors were closed just because he'd rushed things. It didn't mean there was no hope.

It was just in his head—the memory of her looking at him with those bleak-soft eyes. Those I'm-sorry-but-I-can't eyes.

And that McKay-you-lost-her thud in his stomach just kept getting more and more leaden.

Once the night started falling, the light dropped fast, but he didn't want to head in. Not yet. Not before he had some solid plans in his head over what he could say to Lexie next. The sharp, cool air slapped his cheeks and helped him think, and it wasn't like the dusky light mattered. He knew the land the way he knew his own pulse, every root on the path, every downed branch. So he walked.

And kept on walking.

He was trying to outwalk despair, and doing a lousy job of it, when a small critter suddenly crossed the path in a hell-fire hurry to escape the human's presence—meaning him. Any other time, Cash would have been amused by the possum's antics. On this occasion, though, the critter startled him. His boot skidded on something slick. His right knee cracked against something as unyielding as a rock.

And he went down, crashing in the dirt on his rump.

It wasn't the first tumble Cash had ever taken. There was nothing particularly new in an outdoor man having an occasional tussle with the elements. But when he tried to get to his feet, he couldn't.

From a small round window in the lodge library, Lexie could glimpse the top of the climbing wall from over the treetops. Dusk fell while she stood there, remembering how she'd told Cash she had a serious fear of heights…and remembering the morning when he'd insisted she try climbing.

She should have known then what kind of a man he was— the kind who'd throw a woman right in the middle of her worst fears.

And the kind of man who would stand by her…until said-woman figured out whether she wanted to be rescued. Or whether she was strong enough to rescue herself. Or, choice three. Whether she planned to hide out in the lodge library until the next millennium or she found the right words to tell Cash what she desperately wanted to.

She was pretty sure she wanted to pick Choice Three. But it was those sacred right words that weren't coming to her all that fast.

"Lexie?"

She spun around at the unexpected sound of Sammy's voice. There was no reason the whole world couldn't hang out in the library—but no one ever did after dinner—which was why she'd started to think of the room as her private hideaway. She never minded an interruption from Sammy, anyway. She loved him upside and down the other, and she took one look at the beat-up baseball cap and dirt-chewed jeans and almost smiled. Until she saw his expression. "Hey...what's wrong, hon?"

"I can't find Cash. I was playing a game with Keegan, only then I won and went back to our place and Cash wasn't there. I figured he was up here with you, so I waited and waited, 'cause I know you guys can talk forever when you get started. Only now it's getting dark. And he's not here, either?"

"No, I haven't seen him." A quick glance at her watch brought on a frown. "It is a little late—"

"Yeah. Nine. And he's usually on my case about getting ready for bed by eight-thirty." Sammy lifted his shoulders. "Like I could put myself to bed, because I'm so old, you know? Only Cash always says that he can't sleep until he gets a hug, so I usually let him do a good-night thing with me. For his sake and all. Only so far he hasn't come home."

"Sounds to me like you lucked out—you get to stay up late."

"Yeah, I know. Cool, huh?"

"Way cool," Lexie agreed, but she crossed the room in a blink. Sammy had old-man eyes at the moment. She stroked down his cowlick, smiled reassuringly. "I'll tell you

what. How about if we ask Keegan? And if Keegan hasn't
seen Cash, then we could call Bubba, or George. And if they
don't know, I could wander around, ask the people in the
new group who flew in from Omaha. You know your dad
spends a lot of time with newcomers. He probably just got
caught up, talking or doing something with them, you
know?''

"Yeah, I know, and I figured that's where he was, too, if
he wasn't with you. Except not exactly. See, he always finds
me by eight-thirty, Lexie. Always. Lots of times he gets
busy. Lots of times he gets unexpected stuff he has to do.
But he *always* tells me where he is if he's gonna be late.
Even minutes late. Even though I'm so big I can handle it
and all.''

"Sammy." She framed his face with her hands, coaxing
him to still the fidgets for just a couple of seconds. "Nothing's wrong with Cash. Stop worrying. He probably just got
held up, doing something unexpected.''

"I'm not worried. That's just what I thought.''

Those old-man eyes in a little-boy face told her something
else. "Well, look, how about if we go to your place and
watch the tube, and I'll just stay with you until Cash comes
home. We'll make popcorn or something. Okay?''

"Okay.''

Once in Cash's living room, she first turned on lights to
brighten up the place, then tuned in a sitcom for Sammy.
He seemed settled down for a bit, so she scooted into the
minikitchen and a little more private telephone. She managed to rouse both Keegan and Bubba on the first try. Both
men offered to stay with Sammy, but neither expressed the
slightest concern. Maybe Cash had taken a walk or was busy
doing something. Granted, it was unusual for him to be without a pager for Sammy, but things happened. Sammy knew
he could call Keegan or George or Bubba and get help in
two seconds flat. Cash would never have left the property

without communicating with the team. There just wasn't a problem. Wait a bit and he'd undoubtedly show up.

The guys' response reflected reassuring common sense to Lexie but not to Sammy. She mixed up a ginger ale and ice cream to make a Boston Cooler for the squirt, and took that in with a plate of cookies. She'd hoped the treats would distract him, but he didn't even touch the snickerdoodles. That freckled-face still had the worry lines of a CEO with a disturbing quarter report.

"You tried to call Keegan, didn't you?"

"Yes," she said honestly, and curled up on the couch next to Sammy—close enough to be within snuggling distance, but hopefully not so close that she'd make him feel babied. "I also called Bubba and George. George is the only one I couldn't reach…but, Sammy, neither of them seemed at all worried. Everybody knows your dad sometimes gets involved in projects and can forget to look at his watch."

"Yeah, he does. But not when it's my bedtime. He *always* tells me if he's gonna be somewhere else when it's my bedtime."

"I hear you, sport. But I honestly think it's too early to worry. I think we need to give him a little more time to show up. He could be anywhere. And we're staying up, doing just fine in the meantime, right? Besides which…we can really read him a real riot act for being so late when he walks in."

Finally those blue eyes brightened. "Yeah! We'll really yell at him! Boy. He'll be sorry he's so late."

"We'll pin his ears to the wall."

"Yeah, about the ears! We'll level him!"

"We'll tear a strip off his hide for worrying us."

"Yeah! Oh, yeah!" Sammy said exuberantly, but only a few heart-blinks later, he hunched over with his eyes closed. "Lexie…I think I'm having one of your 'xiety attacks. I'm not sure. But my heart keeps beating really hard. And my

hands are all sweaty and icky. And I want to throw up. Is
that how you felt? When you were a little girl locked in that
closet and you were scared for your mom and dad?''

Macho pride or no macho pride, Lexie hooked an arm
around his shoulder and hugged. Hard. ''Yes, sweetheart.
That's exactly how I felt.''

But her eyes suddenly squeezed closed. No one had
punched her—obviously—yet she had the oddest sensation
as if she'd just been slapped, hard. She was trying to help
Sammy, not the other way around, yet the child had so innocently invoked old, dusty emotions that she'd been hiding
in an emotional attic for years now.

Sammy couldn't stand it, the idea of losing Cash. Just
like, years before, she'd been terrorized at the fear of losing
her parents. And what was giving Sammy the symptoms of
a panic attack wasn't loss, but the fear of loss, and that
terrible blind, helpless, unbearable feeling that he couldn't
do anything. And Lexie knew every single corner of that
specific nightmare.

Her heart was suddenly racing, racing. She couldn't stand
it. The fear of losing anyone else she loved. And as if puzzle
pieces all suddenly clicked in place, she realized how much
she'd misunderstood, for so long. All these years, she'd
wanted so badly to fit in, to find a place for herself. All these
years, she'd thought that problem was a flaw in her.

All these years, she'd been wrong.

It wasn't a flaw in her, but a fear in her. Nothing equaled
the anguish of losing her parents. Nothing—even love—
seemed half as important as never having to endure that pain
again.

And she realized before this that she'd fallen deeper than
a sinker for Cash. But not that her love was this strong. So
strong that it brought out all those old, unmanageable fears.

She stroked Sammy's head, ruffling his hair, sensing how
hard he was trying to be brave and hold back tears. And in

her mind, the memories kept battering her awareness. She never had fit in, not because she hadn't been loved as a child, but because she'd never opened the door and allowed it to happen. And the old secret reason was right there. In the smell and memory of that old, dark closet. The desperation of terror and the fury of helplessness, that the people she loved most in life were hurt. And there was nothing she could do about it.

The feeling, then and now, was unbearable.

"Sammy," she said gently, "I know how scary it is. I know. But if there's a way we can find your dad, we will."

"I was afraid you'd say it was late and I had to go to bed."

"No, darlin'. There's no way I'd tell you that. If you're worried, we worry together. And if something's wrong, we stick it out together. Okeydoke?"

"You think he's hurt? Bad hurt?" Tears splashed from Sammy's eyes when he finally got the fear spit out in words.

"I'll be darned if I'll lie to you, honey. I think something must have happened or he'd have called. This just isn't like him and I know you realize that, too. But Sammy, you also know that your dad is one strong, smart cookie. Even if he somehow hurt himself, that doesn't mean he's in trouble he can't get out of."

Sammy thought that over, and then pulled up his knees. She didn't say anything about shoes on the couch. He didn't say anything when she pulled up her knees with her shoes on the couch, either. "I don't remember when my mom took off," he confessed. "I was too little. But sometimes I wake up in the night and I think I remember. I picture it in my mind, even if I know it didn't happen that way. But I think...if I could just have *done* something different, maybe she wouldn't have gone."

"You know what, Sam? That's how I felt, too. About my

mom and dad. As if I'd just had the power to *do* something, I could have made them be all right.''

Sammy nodded vigorously. ''See. That's what bugs me. I keep thinking, maybe it was something about me that made mom take off. Maybe I wasn't a good boy.''

''Aw, Sammy, you dolt.'' She squeezed him double hard this time. ''You couldn't be more wrong, you goof. You're a boy that any mom would dream about having. You're that special, that wonderful. And I don't want to embarrass you to death, but I just want you to know. You're a terrific kid and I love you. I only wish you were my son.''

''Cripes. Cut it out.''

''Sorry.''

''Cash gets corny like that, too, sometimes. It's disgusting.''

''I understand.'' She brushed the tears from under his eyes. Then from under her eyes. ''I'll try not to say anything embarrassing again.''

''Good. Like, I love you, too, Lex, but that doesn't mean we have to *talk* about it.''

''Gotcha.'' She hesitated. ''But can I tell you one more thing?''

''If it isn't so mushy.''

''It's not mushy. It's about your worrying about Cash tonight. I think he's going to walk in the door any minute. I really do. But...you know the way you felt, about having no power over your mom disappearing?''

''Yeah.''

''And that's the same way I felt. About having no power about my mom and dad disappearing from my life. It's an orphan thing, that I'm not sure other people understand like we do.'' Finally she saw him taking a sip of the Boston Cooler. ''But the thing is...like tonight. When Cash isn't there for a few minutes. You and I are more inclined to worry more than most people, you know? Because of what we've been through."

"Yeah, I get you."

"And because we can't stand it. Feeling like we don't have any power to help. Like we don't have a choice. Like there's nothing we can do."

"Yeah, Lexie! Exactly! It makes you just want to pound a wall, you know? Or I guess, if you're a girl, it could make you want to cry."

Lexie figured that eventually she'd have to tackle Sammy on his sexist thinking, but this just wasn't the time. Temporarily he was all settled down again, munching on snickerdoodles, kicked back on a mound of pillows, content enough. But when the clock ticked past ten—and then ten-thirty—those tears started to well on him again.

She called Keegan again, but except for offering to come over and sit with Sammy, Keegan had nothing new to say. It had been too dark for hours for anyone to attempt to search outside. Come daylight, if Cash still hadn't shown up, Keegan would lead some troops. "I hear you, Lexie. You want to stay with Sammy, that's super, but just both of you go to sleep, okay? Remember how big the property is. He's only been gone a couple of hours. Relax. He just got caught up doing something."

Around eleven, Martha scratched on the door. Heaven knew where she'd left her puppies—probably in Lexie's room—but the dog had come in to mope with the two of them.

"Look," she told Sammy finally. "Nobody thinks there's a problem but you and me, Sammy. But you know what?"

"What?"

"We'll both feel better if we have a plan, that's what. We really can't go out looking for him. It's too dark. That wouldn't even make sense. But how about if we bunk down on the couch together here. Then if Cash comes in, we'll both be right here and wake up at the same time. And if he doesn't, then we'll be ready to go out and start searching for him at the first light of dawn. How's that for a plan?"

"Sounds good to me."

Sammy dropped off within minutes after that. She covered him with an extra blanket, switched off the lights except for one soft lamp in the far corner and then paced. From corner to corner. Window to window.

She was worried about Cash…but not too worried. Logical or not, she was positive that somehow she'd have known if he were in really dire trouble. What weighed on her heart, though, was his asking to marry her.

She hadn't believed him.

That he could really mean it.

That he could believe she fit in his life—and Sammy's.

That he could really love the misfit Alexandra Jeannine Woolf.

Around two in the morning the stars were so brilliant that the woods seemed painted with silver moonshine. Dew rose, putting a diamond glisten on everything green. All wind died.

Slowly, though, the stars started to blur. Slowly the sharp edges of the moon softened. Slowly the midnight sky lightened from that heavy, weightless black to a dustier black velvet, then to dusky charcoal. Then came the first birdsong, even before the mist of dawn.

By the time the sky turned pearl-gray, she'd changed clothes and laced up Sammy's old shoes and put together granola and fruit for the two of them. Sammy woke up with a start. He headed for the bathroom, fast, but within minutes they were both ready to peel outside and start looking.

"You really meant it, didn't you, Lexie?" he asked her. "About staying with me all night. About searching with me. About believing me about Cash needing us."

"Yes. I meant it all." Considering she'd had a sleepless

night, she wasn't sure where the odd, strong feeling of power came from.

It was the feeling of powerlessness that she'd never been able to stand. And this last night, worried Cash was hurt, had certainly made her and Sammy both feel powerless...at least technically. Only it wasn't the same, and Lexie was positive that the old nightmare could never haunt her again.

She loved him. That was the difference. She had power on the inside, from loving him and being loved by him—a difference she'd never understood before.

Cash was all right.

She willed him to be all right.

Cash couldn't say it was the most fun walk he'd ever taken, but once he'd found a sturdy, usable walking stick, he knew he could at least make it home. The knee hurt like a witch. He'd seen too many wilderness injuries to fear there was a break or anything that serious. This was nothing that Bubba couldn't probably pummel or doctor out of him, more like a deep-bone bruise that was going to heal on its own annoying long time.

For damn sure, though, there'd been no way he could have made it home in the dark—not without risking more injury. Giving the knee a few hours rest with the limb elevated had eased the swelling as well.

As the sun stole over the horizon, though, Cash was hungry, thirsty, hurting and aggravated. He hated being absentee for Sammy. The kid had caretakers over at Silver Mountain, but that wasn't the point. Sammy had a real fear about being left, which was why Cash never took off without telling the squirt where he was and when he'd be back. So the kid had undoubtedly had a rough night, and there was nothing Cash could do about it.

He felt bad about Sammy. But the dread lunging through his pulse was about Lexie being left alone all night.

She feared being left, too.

Just like Sammy. Only her fear was adult-size, her night-mares woman-colored. Over the long, lonely night, studying the black sky, Cash finally figured out the Big Thing that hounded her so badly. The Thing that gave her the shake attacks. The Thing that made her scared instead of happy when the wild idea that someone could love her surfaced.

It was about her losing her parents, way back. It was about her loving so much, so deeply, that fear of losing again just plain had her terrorized. Same damn thing Sammy did.

Well, Cash had had enough of it.

They were going to talk it out when he got home. Yell it out, if they had to. He wasn't leaving her. She was just going to have to get that through her stubborn, curly head. And she was marrying him—and Sammy. Or she was going to have a damn good reason why not.

He was scowling when he turned a corner and that slight twisting motion shot knife-spears of pain up his thigh. Possibly he'd yell at her just a little later. Possibly not the precise instant he got home. Possibly…

Hells bells, there they were. At the high tilt in the path, hiking side by side, heads together. And then they both looked up. And saw him. And started running.

Cash almost—almost—hustled to meet them halfway. But then he mentally kicked himself, realizing that was a wrong thing to do. Instead he stopped and leaned heavily on his walking stick and did his best to look pitiful.

The squirt's eyes were glistening when he threw himself under Cash's arm and squeezed his waist. But Lexie…oh man. Lexie looked up at him with those exotic dark eyes full of love, and said fiercely, "Damn you, McKay. Don't you ever scare us like that again."

"I was hurt—" he started to say.

"We *knew* you were hurt. Come on, we'll get you home. Sammy, you take his left side." She hurled away his walking stick, which was not, truth to tell, the best of ideas. Sammy was a half-pint and she wasn't the sturdiest support in town herself.

But he was figuring it out, fast now, that his two loved ones needed to help him. They needed the power of coming through for him, and if he was hunky-dory fine, they would never have the chance to show off their hero power. Actually, even if he'd wanted to reassure them that he was okay, Lexie was yelling at him so steadily that he could barely get in a word.

"I have to go back, for at least three weeks. It's not just business. I can move my business. Everything you said before is true—in this day of faxes and modems, I could really do my type of work from anywhere. It's just that it'll take some time to get the changes started and set in motion. Also, I *do* want to keep some office space in the city—don't argue with me!"

"Okay," he said meekly.

"There are just times I'll have to fly in. Cut-and-dried. And it would be ridiculously dumb to give up my work when it's going so well. So don't argue with me about that, either."

"Okay," he said meekly.

"Sammy needs exposure to some civilization and sophistication, besides."

"What? No, I don't—" Sammy piped up, clearly aghast at this turn in the conversation.

"Yes, he does," Lexie insisted to Cash. "He needs to see plays, hear music, expand his educational opportunities. So, I think it's obvious that all of us want Silver Mountain to be our home base. But I expect both of you to compromise, and not give me a bunch of grief over the times I'm going to push some city life on both of you."

"Okay, Lexie." Cash winked at Sammy.

"I get it, Cash! Okay, Lexie! Okay!" Sammy echoed.

"Furthermore, you'll both be wearing tuxes for the wedding."

"Weddi—?" Sammy looked at him. Cash just nodded and made a motion for him to be quiet.

"I've got a lot of family," Lexie continued full tilt with her harangue. "You have to meet all of them. Frankly you're both likely to love 'em more than me. They'll love everything about all the outside stuff around Silver Mountain. But Sammy—I'm warning you now, the women will all mom-you and love-you half to death. You'll have to live with it."

Sammy looked at Cash, and sighed heavily. "I guess I can bear up."

"And another thing—"

She had about fifty more "and another things." Sweat beaded on Cash's forehead from the effort of walking. But around a half mile from the house, Lexie stopped hiking and ranting both. She ordered Sammy to run and get Keegan, have Keegan bring the Jeep so that Cash could ride the rest of the way.

So that was the last he had to walk. And the pain neutralized when he could quit with the exercise and just stand motionless again. Still, the instant Sammy took off, Lexie suddenly lifted her face and looked at him.

Seconds before, birds had been singing like maniacs and squirrels cavorting all over the place. Now, there was suddenly silence. All he could hear was his heart pounding, and all he could see were those eyes of hers, so soft, so suddenly vulnerable and wary.

"When I get you home alone, McKay, do you know what I want to do to you?"

"I sure hope so," he said fervently.

There. A smile. Just before he hauled her straight into his arms and wrapped her up, tight as a bow. "I'm *never* going to lose you, Cash," she said fiercely.

"I knew that. I just wasn't positive if you did."

"I love you." Her voice was muffled in his throat, partly because it seemed he couldn't stand to let her go, even for a second. "My whole heart's worth."

"Aw, Lexie. I love you, heart and soul. If it's up to me, I promise you the best of what I am, for all our days together, for all our lives."

Eventually they broke apart—but not willingly, and only when they both heard the rumbling engine of the Jeep and knew they were about to be interrupted. Still, they came together for one last kiss—a kiss that sealed all the promises for the future they wanted to make together. And then they smiled, hooked hands and waited for Sammy to bound out of the Jeep to join them.

* * * * *

Jennifer Greene launches
Silhouette Desire's brand-new
TEXAS CATTLEMAN CLUB'S
continuity with

DR. MILLIONAIRE.

Don't miss this special book,
on sale January 2001
from Silhouette Desire.

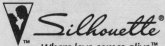